THE FAN

I was wearing a thin
almost as soft as chiffon. He came over to me and
put his hands on my shoulders, then ran them
down lightly, round the circles of my breasts. Slim,
sun-tanned hands, hands that knew where they
wanted to go. His fingers took the top button of the
blouse and undid it, and the next one, then slipped
inside and nestled round my breasts. He squeezed a
little, then relaxed. Then he took the nipples
between his fingers and worked them this way and
that, making them tingle and swell till they felt as if
they might burst out in fountains of juice. I
couldn't wait, my fingers were at his belt...

THE FANTASY HUNTERS

Celeste Arden

A Nexus Book
published by
the Paperback Division of
W.H. Allen & Co Plc

A Nexus Book
Published in 1989
by the Paperback Division of
W.H. Allen & Co Plc
175/9 St. John Street, London EC1V 4LL

Printed and bound in Great Britain by
Courier International Ltd, Tiptree, Essex

ISBN 0 352 32413 9

Chapters

1

Flying

The difficulty is to stop the other passengers from seeing
my hand moving up and down under the blanket. The
aisles are narrow even in Club Class, and the man
opposite with the knowing eyes keeps catching mine,
although I look away every time. The blanket is brown,
felty, and large enough to cover me and my neighbour.
My fingers explore his cock, and I feel a warm surge
between them. It is still growing, it grows huge.

I concentrate on the crack of light showing under the
blind. It is still sunny out there in Abovecloudland,
though the cabin is lit only with the flickering light from
the film. I can just see the blanket undulating, and his
closed eyelids. Asleep perhaps? I think not, because he
smiles and murmurs something. I can't hear because of
the noise from the engine.

I did not expect my first assignment to be so
straightforward. You can easily find yourself next to
another woman even in the smoker's seats, and if you get
a man he may not turn out to be compliant. Still, I
thought a ten-hour flight would give a man, even a
married one, time to get horny. Was I ever right?

As it turned out, the plane was only half full, and we

could all choose where to sit. I chose an aisle seat next to one in a green and white shirt and beige belted trousers. He got up and offered me his place by the window. I took it without saying anything. Silence all through taxiing and take-off. I looked down at his light trousers. They seemed tight at the crotch, with a promising bulge. Perhaps it was just the effect of the ludicrous position of the seats which aircraft designers impose on humanity.

Up in the air he turned to me and smiled. 'I'm glad that's over – I always want to pray just before take-off. Silly, that. I didn't pray regular since I was a kid.' The voice was American, with those long Southern vowels, but with a practical edge to it. I practised a sympathetic smirk on him, and got a cigarette in exchange. As he leaned over to light it I took in his sun-tanned face. Mouth a bit loose at the corners, ready to twist into a smile. Or a kiss, I imagined. You're going to be a pushover, I thought. 'Do you travel alone much?' I said.

'I reckon maybe ten, twelve times a year. I have business in Europe, mostly London England.'

'That's a lot of lonely travelling.'

'I don't know. You can get lucky and find yourself sitting next to a real pretty woman. That's some kind of consolation.'

'I know the feeling. Sometimes I find myself next to a dark, handsome stranger, and then I forget what time it is.'

'What time is it, then?'

'Now, now! Time for supper, look. They're bringing it round.'

In a moment our small shared cubicle of space was filled with a confusion of plastic trays, dishes, cups, knives, forks, glasses. Horrid little plastic jars of

8

chemicals for whitening your coffee, guaranteed to contain absolutely no milk or other natural substance.

'Plastic food too on this airline. But the wine's okay. The stuff from California has gotten quite drinkable. I'll get the stewardess to leave us the bottle.'

I looked at his eyes while he flashed them at her. 'Watch yourself with this one, sweetheart. He's a bit of a bastard' I thought. Well, he got the bottle, and another one later while they were clearing up all the plastic. Then they turned on the film and made us all lower the blinds. We hadn't plugged in the headphones, so I couldn't make head or tail of the plot. One problem is that if you can't hear the actors' voices you can't tell them apart.

'I think I'll take a nap,' he said. 'I've had that movie on my last two trips over, and it's the most God-awful crap about some cocaine bust.'

'It must be hell for the cabin staff, having to watch the same film over and over again.'

'Don't you believe it! They're all back there in a little caboose they have. Two hours off cabin duty, and the best screwing of any airline bar the old TWA.'

His voice was powerful, but he made it caress me suggestively. He reached out his blanket and draped it over him, but I could see his eyes were still open as the light flickered on them from the screen.

'If you want to nap too you'll be needing a blanket.'

'They don't seem to have given me one.' I lied. I had hidden it under my seat an hour back.

'Figure on sharing with me?'

'OK. Thanks, I will.'

'Atta girl! Guess if we move this arm-rest there'd be more room for us both.'

He pushed back the dividing arm flush with the seats,

9

and we both leaned back. It was time to begin my research. I moved my hand, ever so lightly, and it rested against his thigh. It felt taut and trembled, I thought, at the touch. The plane lurched suddenly – turbulence. As it heaved again, I let my hand skid across his thigh towards his lap, as if I'd been unbalanced by the plane's shaking. I was prepared to withdraw it and apologise, but a strong, warm hand grasped mine firmly and held it, and then moved it downwards slightly until it rested on a long, firm bulge.

I had been looking straight ahead, eyes half-closed, as if the adventures of my hand were no responsibility of mine, but now I turned towards the stranger and met his eyes. He smiled and raised his eyebrows and then, silently, his mouth formed the word 'Please.' I nodded.

I turned round towards the aisle and hunched myself under the blanket, as if to settle down to sleep. The stranger brought my hand up to his belt, then guided it down his zip, then pushed it firmly inside the gap. Down there was a new world, a chaotic jungle of sensual life. First I felt a satiny texture – silk underpants – and then a hot, humid forest of hair. Pulsing in its depths was a long, lithe nocturnal beast, which leapt towards my hand and pressed against it. I took the tip between my fingers, then ran them slowly down the shaft. It was infected by the moistness and heat around it, and felt damp against my dry fingers. The shaft seemed to stretch for ever as my finger travelled slowly down in the darkness. The journey ended in a soft roundness, and the stranger's balls contracted beneath the touch. I made an exploration of these too. In the dark, operating by touch alone, everything assumes gigantic proportions, we know – but I swear that these were the largest balls I had ever felt. I could barely cradle them in my hand. As I did so, the stranger sighed and leant back, closing his eyes. I had a co-operative subject.

And so, my only obstacle, or difficulty, is to stop the blanket moving, to make sure that the prying or prurient eyes of my fellow-passengers see not a twitch or a quiver. I nestle down further, and heave the blanket up on my shoulder, making a sort of tent in which my hand and arm can move freely. My fingers play a drumming tune on the tip of the stranger's cock, tapping lightly, then squeezing gently. I roll the foreskin down, then back, down then back, in a slow rhythm. The unseen cock seems to wave about with pleasure, in jerky movements beyond the owner's control. Now I take the whole length of it in my hand and give it lingering, undulating squeezes, working from tip to root. Squeezing is hard – you might as well try to compress an iron bar – but my hand delights in the cauldron-heat and the firmness of the beast – as it, too, seems to delight in its handler.

Excitement takes over. In my own body, somewhere, far away, I feel an urgent throbbing which starts between my legs and sends the message to my brain – 'I want it inside me!' But it's not so easy to join the Five-Mile High Club as its soi-disant members claim. If I were to climb on top of the stranger everyone would see, or guess. No good. And the way I feel now, it would be impossible to stop the blanket from heaving until it slipped off us both and revealed our disgrace. Besides, I'm wearing jeans – so stupid, I tell myself. So my brain sends a message back down – 'Not now. Later perhaps. Wait.' But the throbbing grows faster as I run my fingers up and down the unknown cock.

The man beside me is moving now, turning slightly

11

from side to side, arching his back, pressing his head against the head-rest, smiling to himself. I know why, because I am twisting his organ fiercely from side to side. My other hand has joined in now, and is holding his scrotum, kneading his pulsating balls in the same fierce rhythm. The heat under the blanket increases and inside the stranger's most secret parts it reaches boiling point. All at once, it boils over – a mighty leap of the imprisoned beast, and scalding liquid courses through my fingers and on to my palms. The stranger jerks upright, once, twice, then falls back. Instead of crying out, he has held his breath, and now he breathes long and hard, open-mouthed, and shudders perceptibly.

His hand finds mine and strokes it slowly, with an unexpected tenderness. He opens his eyes and looks down at me as I lie under the blanket. 'Thank you,' he whispers, then he closes them slowly in contentment. I sit up again, until I am leaning back, touching his shoulder with mine but not quite leaning on it. Our tent collapses. I risk looking round at the aisle. The man in the opposite row, now wearing headphones, is looking straight at me – accusingly, but who cares now? The loud, urgent message from between my legs is quieter, and though I can still feel a slow pulse there and a dampness, I'm too tired to think about it.

Four Days Later
I've been in New Orleans for three days, and there's lots to report. But there's also more to say about the journey here. I thought when I went to sleep just over the American shore, that my project with the stranger had ended. I must have slept for a few hours. I was dreaming,

12

I think, of being one of a pair of writhing, naked bodies, floating out from the plane window into a blue sky like tepid water, when the next thing I knew was that someone was touching my shoulder and saying 'Is your belt fastened? We're just going to touch down in Houston. By the way, my name is Robert – what's yours?'

I opened my eyes. The plane was bright now. We had flown into the afternoon, and everything was brilliant with golden light. Robert was bending towards me, his eyes very bright and intense. I almost forgot my name, then remembered it.

'I'm Justine.'

'Well, Justine, it's sure nice to have met with you. I really enjoyed this flight.'

He was going to add something when the screaming of the engine as we dropped the last few hundred yards made hearing impossible, so he sat back and took my hand, and stroked the palm with one finger as we touched down and taxied towards the airport buildings. Then there was the usual bustle and jostle of seven hundred people trying to be first off the plane. Our seats were at the back, so we sat and waited. People slammed the lockers and surged forward. Robert said quietly, 'Since it's a five-hour wait for the connection, could we spend the time together?'

I found myself saying, more eagerly than I intended, 'That would be lovely. But where shall we go? It's too far to get to town and back in time.'

He laughed and winked and said 'I know a little place nearby. Just come with me.'

Finally we left the plane and shuffled through all the formalities, and then Robert picked up my bag with one hand and held mine tight with the other – as if I would run away, which I had no thought of doing – and took me down an elevator to an underground lobby. The light here was dreamlike – there were no shadows and we were quite alone. Robert bent down and gave me a long, questing kiss. Then a metallic Texan voice barked at us:

'THE PEOPLE-MOVER WILL ARRIVE IN HALF A MINUTE. PLEASE STAND CLEAR OF THE DOORS.'

The lobby was a subway station in an airport dreamworld. The People-mover swooped up noiselessly and collected us, then glided on. The metal voice grated in my ears.

'PLEASE PUT YOUR BAGGAGE IN A SAFE PLACE. STANDING PASSENGERS PLEASE HOLD ON. NEXT STOP, THE MARRIOTT HOTEL. HAVE A NICE DAY.'

The Marriott Hotel lobby was palatial and impersonal, full of sumptuous leather armchairs for people with time to while away. Robert went to the reception and paid for a short-stay room. He seemed to know his way around, and led me to the elevator. It had a glass side, and suddenly we rose above the lightless levels of People-mover and Reception and saw a garden and a bright-blue pool, surrounded by flowering shrubs. We got out and walked round the corridor, for the hotel was circular, until we found 109. Robert opened the door and I hesitated – was this really what I wanted? But he pushed me gently inside and chained the door.

'It's OK. Nobody will bother us here. I ordered some wine and food, but they'll leave it outside for us if we're busy.'

The room had two queen-sized beds and dark, heavy

curtains. Outside all round us was the airport. The hotel was an oasis in the middle of the tarmac and the screeching planes, but the windows were completely soundproof and all that you noticed of the airport was the mechanical pantomine of landings, taxiings and take-offs. Robert came to the window and drew the curtains across. The room was softly lit by a small lamp at the desk, and a large mirror facing the beds diffused the light further. Robert stood between the two beds.

'You know, you're something else,' he said, and laughed. 'I'd always had a fantasy of being tossed off in a plane by a beautiful blonde.'

'You could do it yourself, I suppose. Much easier.'

'Depends who you're sitting next to. I usually travel with one of my junior executives.'

'And none of them are blonde?'

'You're joking! They're all Grecian-2000 black, and old before their time.'

There was a knock at the door and a clattering outside. Robert went to open the door, and took in a tray with a champagne bucket and sandwiches. He uncorked the bottle and gave me a glass, then said: 'I invited you here because I really want your help – I want to live out one of my wildest fantasies. But listen – if you don't want to join in, it's no sweat. We can just eat something and have a swim.'

'What's your fantasy?'

'I guess it's rather banal. I'm forty-five, I'm married, with two kids. I'm happy. I'll stay that way. I just want to have the sexiest four hours of my life with a total stranger – a woman I'll never see again.'

'The sexiest four hours? It's a tall order, but – let's try!'

I was wearing a thin blouse, tucked down the front, almost as soft as chiffon. He came over to me and put his hands on my shoulders, then ran them down lightly, round the circles of my breasts. Slim, sun-tanned hands, hands that knew where they wanted to go. His fingers took the top button of the blouse and undid it, and the next one, then slipped inside and nestled round my breasts. He squeezed a little, then relaxed. Then he took the nipples between his fingers and worked them this way and that, making them tingle and swell till they felt as if they might burst out in fountains of juice. I couldn't wait, my fingers were at his belt and undoing it, then at his flies. My hands dug down swiftly into the familiar hot jungle of hair and soft flesh and found his cock, urging itself against them, sticky still from our last encounter. I caressed it between my fingertips while he sighed and his hands on my nipples relaxed. He bent and kissed my lips – he was trembling.

'Jesus,' he breathed, 'don't let's hang around.'

Then he was throwing off his jacket and shirt. I stood and watched, and soon he was naked in front of me. He was lean, and very brown from the sun, and sweating heavily. The light picked out the shining muscles on his chest and arms in relief – but my eyes were drawn down to where his ready cock rose up towards me, waving with its fullness and tension. He came over, turned me round to face the mirror and unbuttoned the last buttons of my blouse, reaching over from behind. He pulled it aside, so that I could see my tits reflected – apricot-coloured in the dim light, and now circled between his brown hands. Then he slipped his hands down to my waist and slowly, confidently, inside my trousers. His palms were against my belly, pressing downwards until he touched the edge

16

of my curling hair. The trousers were loose at the waist and he pulled them down until I stood naked too, seeing myself in his eyes in the mirror.

Blonde hair in long waves which spread over my shoulders, breasts like large pomegranates, dark-flushed nipples. A curving belly leading down to a crescent moon of pale hair. His arms now gripped me firmly round my waist while his hands went below and burrowed into the crescent moon, touching at last – to my relief – the tiny sharp tip of flesh there. Fingers curled downwards and inwards until they found the lips of my cunt and softly prised them apart to dig inside. I was wet – his fingers felt my oil and skated along the soft membranes, stopping to explore the mouth of my cunt. I closed my eyes and shivered.

Now he turned me round to face him and pressed his hard muscles and still bulging cock against my belly, while his hands ran over my buttocks and delved briefly into the secret crevice there. Then, lightly and easily, he hooked his arms round me and lifted me on to the bed and pressed his whole body against me with desperate force. My legs drifted apart of their own volition. He twisted between them and I felt the smooth length of his cock lying along my outer lip, like a sun-basking snake. My cunt-lips were gorged with blood and, way beyond any choice of mine, opened themselves and kissed the stranger's cock, warmly and wetly. It jerked wildly, then moved along my lips, up and down, asking for admission, until its knob rested on the entrance to my inner parts. This gaped wide now in welcome and suddenly, with a swift turn, his great prick swam into the welcoming cave – so far in the first rush that it thrust against my womb and rested there.

17

My heart was leaping, the more so because my lover moved his head to suckle my nipples, and laced his hands at my waist to pull me on to him. I felt the trembling of his haunches as he almost came at the first entry, and then he shuddered and stopped himself. But my cunt was throbbing, avid for his thrusting, and soon it started. Each movement of his was like an explosion inside me. I cried out every time he touched the heart of me. He panted and gripped me fiercely, then rotated his cock in a swerving spiral which made the sweat pour down my arms and the juice out between my legs. So wild and joyous was the sensation that I screamed once. At that, he twisted me on his shaft twice more and I melted completely, and shouted out my joy.

The pleasure of my dissolution sent him into a frenzy of thrusting. His cock grew mightier still and rammed itself against the gate of my womb. His head butted against my breasts and his whole body was taut as a bowstring. His cock moved into me again and seemed to stretch my cunt to bursting point. Then there was a moment of quiet, a sudden, deceptive softening of the iron rod, before it made a mighty surge, then another, and flooded me with its spunk. He was groaning and he thrust onto me again and again before he was done. Then he collapsed on top of me, whispering 'Sweet, sweet fuck!'

Time must have passed, for the sun was slanting low into the room behind the curtains. I woke to find the stranger's hands running over my flanks and kneading my buttocks, while he forced his whole body against mine again, so I could feel that his prick was already long and stiff. Hardly recalling where I was, or who I was with, I curled my arms round his neck and asked

18

dreamily, 'Can we do it again?'

'Let's do it another way this time,' he said. I opened my eyes and saw that he was smiling.

'How do you want to do it?'

'Come with me.' He raised me to my feet and led me towards the bathroom. It was tiled in dark blue, and only dimly lit by a red night light. The bath was huge and deep. We stepped into it, half-entwined, and my stranger switched on the shower, and turned to me. In the strange, glowing light his face and body had a savage look and his cock rose towards me again, casting a threatening shadow on his hips. For a moment I was half afraid of this new stranger, but he took my shoulders and pulled me into the shower. As the warm drops soaked our hair and skin, he caressed me all over my back and shoulders.

'Now I'll wash you,' he said, still smiling. 'You must be very dirty after that awful plane journey.'

Taking the soap he started the sexiest massage I've ever had. He picked up each foot in turn and pulled the soap between every toe, round the sole, then rubbed it up the back of my legs, stopping short at my bum. The same, then, with the inside of my calves and my thighs, but leaving off before he reached my cunt-hair. Turning me round, he soaped my shoulders and back with strong movements. I was soon filled with excitement, waiting and hoping for him to reach down further. At last, he held my buttocks firmly, one in each hand, and soaped them too, rotating them together. Lust and warmth washed through me. I was light in the head with excitement and desire as he pulled me to face him. The water splashed over us unregarded. With soap on each hand, and keeping me at arm's length, he sculpted my breasts in lather, delicately but deliberately. Moving them first together, then holding them apart, he started a dancing rhythm in my blood which seemed to beat inside my head and my cunt simultaneously. As he did it, he talked urgently.

'You want me to wash your pussy, don't you? But it's smothered in my spunk, so I won't. Instead, I'll just keep on soaping these great, luscious tits of yours until I wash them right away. Do you want to touch my prick now?' I was reaching out for it, but he moved back, still holding me at the end of his arms. 'I bet you do, but you can't. Next time you feel my prick it will be right up inside you, just you wait.'

Whatever else he said I never heard, because he was fondling my belly and pressing himself against my tits, squashing them, holding me close now again. I was frenzied with the need to have him. I reached out towards his cock, but he shook his head. He made me sit on the edge of the bath and knelt in front of me, holding me up as I swayed backwards. His great tool slid between my thighs as he leant towards me and tickled my tenderest spot with it. 'I didn't soap your clit by hand,' he said 'so I'll do it this way instead.' Tantalisingly and softly, his knob worked on my clitoris, rubbing the hood up and down, teasing the tip, which poked out further from its hiding place with every stroke. His cock liked the exercise, and danced up and down. The sharp thrill between my legs grew so electric that I begged him to enter me before it was too late. Suddenly for me it was too late, as I felt the spasm spread out across my stomach – shock waves from that tiny, powerful epicentre. He held me tight then, and waited for a few moments until I was still again. After I had stopped shaking, he pushed his cock past my still throbbing clitoris and into the gaping mouth behind. I thought he had already satiated me, but he delivered strong strokes which awoke my appetite in an instant.

I was hungry for his thrusts. Kneeling in front of me, and holding me as I moved with his strokes, he drove into me very fast, while I shook uncontrollably. The long, smooth length of him reached up into me, again and again, and a warm, perilous sensation washed through my vagina. I felt spent, but I could not quell this new flood of passion and I moved with him eagerly, awaiting and anticipating each new incursion into the centre of my being. At last, he gasped out 'Come now, or I will,' and screwed himself in and out of me like a spiralling storm. The storm broke, and I was shouting out and crying as the thundering spasms wrenched at my cunt. He could not wait an instant longer, and while my vagina still squeezed him like a trap, he squirted a great river of spunk into me, and then thrust twice more until another floodtide came which emptied him entirely.

I fell forward, arms draped over his shoulders, and his head was buried in my breasts. The strong, animal smell of his sweat and his sperm welled up around me and was like a musky perfume. We hung together for a minute. Then we started to stroke each other's backs, tenderly almost. He muttered, 'I never thought it could be like that.' He was kissing my tits and I felt his desire rising against me once more – then the telephone rang in the bedroom. 'Hot damn,' he muttered. He got up and went to it, said a few words, and came back and helped me to stand up.

'That was the alarm call. You have forty minutes to get to your plane.'

'My plane? But I thought that you were going to New Orleans too.'

He looked embarrassed for a second, then smiled broadly. 'Well, I am. But the truth is that I don't travel till Thursday. I have to be here for a meeting tomorrow morning. I have a room reserved in the downtown Four Seasons for tonight. But I figured you'd never come into town for a just a few hours. So I said that I was waiting here as well.'

We both laughed, and he hugged me.

'I guessed that I'd miss out on you altogether unless I played this trick.'

'I'm glad you did. Was it worth it?'

'It was just like my fantasy – just like, but so much better.'

We went back to the bed and started to dress. He gave me some more champagne and I drank it in a gulp, although I already felt light-headed, and was floating in pleasure.

'I think I'll stay here another half-hour and shave. And maybe take another shower. But it won't be so good without you. Honest, you are the most wonderful dame.'

'It was fun. Thanks to you.'

'I guess we won't be meeting in New Orleans. You said you were all tied up there – me too.'

'That's right.'

'What do you do, by the way?'

'Didn't I tell you? I'm a sex researcher.'

His eyes opened wide and he gasped. For a split second he looked horrified, and suddenly, totally vulnerable. Then – as if I could see the inner screen of his brain – I saw him decide not to believe me. He laughed loudly, inordinately.

'Well, you're a deep one, Justine. Whatever you do, good luck to you, and take care. And – hey! – thank you, thanks a million.'

I was moving to the door, but he held me for a moment and kissed my forehead, then my lips. I toyed with the idea of postponing my flight till the next day. It was the most tempting moment of my life, just for a moment. But I opened the door, said goodbye and closed it behind me. Walking round the circular passage to the glass elevator, I felt almost normal again. The noise of planes revving up made me realise that I had to hurry. The elevator sank past the garden pool, dark blue now in the evening sun, with red bougainvilleas brilliant at the margins, then dropped towards the People-mover level. I was on my way to New Orleans. I never thought that my first assignment would be so easy.

Dear Celeste,   *New Orleans*

Here's a report on my first 'interview'. Hope they're all as much fun as this one! Do you like the style? I think that writing might be my métier, really!! Can't stay to write more now, because I'm off to eat at a fancy restaurant with tables on the sidewalk – classy guys sitting out there, looks like a good hunting ground! Please cable me an extra $500 for expenses here – this town swallows dollars like a one-armed bandit swallows dimes!

Love to you all – hope the Project is getting under way and that the girls are meeting lots of tasty men!!!
Yours,
Justine

2

The New Recruit

Celeste Arden throws down the sheaf of pages with a
gesture of disgust. 'What a load of crap! Far too literary.
Justine must think she's an erotic novelist or something.
What we need are some facts!'

She leans back in the leather chair and stretches her
legs out. They already extend half-way across the desk
and her purple thigh boots contrast pleasingly with its
ebony surface – as she no doubt knows. Celeste lights a
cigarette and contemplates the wispy smoke rising
through the sunlight. The black venetian blinds which
shield her from the curiosity of passers-by outside are
half open and rays of afternoon sun push through the
slats, illuminating the room. The room is an Aladdin's
cave of objects and pictures. One wall is a collage of
masks, strange wooden tubes – primitive instruments,
perhaps? – and devices which look like early artisans'
tools, yet defy identification. Part of the long wall facing
the window is covered with sketches and photographs. If
you look closely, you see that these all have something in
common. They depict the more esoteric parts of the
human body, male and female, from unusual angles and
in close-up. Giant balls swell out towards you, tastefully

tinted sepia, and a vulva blown up to the size of a marrow and turned sideways, smiles at you. The photography is so good that you see droplets of moisture on it, which catch the flashlight.

A close-up of Celeste shows her to be long and thin, but voluptuous in parts. Since she is wearing no skirt, her black tights show her outstretched thighs to advantage – well-padded inside, but straight and muscled from the hips downwards. She is wearing a man's shirt, stolen from a theatre wardrobe, you might think, because it has ruffles down the front and wide, sweeping sleeves which gather to a frill at the wrist. It's the sort of shirt in which film stars of the thirties fought duels, and won. The shirt reaches down a long way, but as Celeste twists about irritably in her chair it rides up and you see what might be a flicker of tawny hair beneath the sheer, black tights.

Behind Celeste's chair is a wall full of bookshelves and in the centre of her library, an arched door, half open, leading to a room behind which is dimly, redly lit. Many of the books have lurid covers, but they are all neatly arranged, and the shelves are labelled systematically – MASTURBATION, followed by NECROPHILIA, then ORGASMS, then PERVERSIONS, run the shelves on the right of the door. A voice speaks from the far end of the room. 'Kinsey says that nearly 20 per cent of single rural males have had orgasms with animals by the age of 25.'

At this end of the room is a long sofa, covered with black velvet. On it lounges a young man of startling beauty. He has an ivory skin and fine, fierce features. His hair is jet black, long at the sides. He wears a black T-shirt and tight, black trousers which show his crotch as a promising bulge. He is reading a heavy volume – *Sexual*

Behaviour In The Human Male – in a half-hearted fashion. He riffles through the pages with one hand, while the other drapes languidly over the end of the sofa. You might think he was half asleep if it were not for the sudden intense flash of his dark eyes when he looks at Celeste.

'Remarkable! But we can't include that in the research project. It's illegal in so many countries that nobody will ever own up. Anyway, that's not the sort of thing that men fantasise about, is it?'

'Sure they do. I often have a dream that I'm being stalked through the jungle by a great, sleek tiger. I know that if he catches up with me, he'll rape me.'

'How do you know it's not a she-tiger?'

'Because sometimes he does catch me.' Celeste leans forward and makes a note on a pad. She looks pensive. 'Are dreams the same as fantasies? We've got to sort that out right at the start.'

The doorbell rings, and the young man jumps up with sudden, animal grace and goes out through the dim red room. Celeste listens to the conversation in the passage beyond.

'I'm sorry, she's terribly busy this afternoon.'

'But she said I could call any time after two o'clock.'

'Could I have your name, please? I'll check with her.'

'Lilac Petrosian.'

Celeste calls out.

'That's all right, Ivo. She has an appointment.'

Ivo shows the new arrival in. She is tall, even Junoesque, with a mass of bushy, wavy, brown hair, which falls over her shoulders and touches the tips of her high, firm breasts. Her mouth is pert and red and – just now – twisted in a nervous smile. She wears a long, tight, rust-coloured silk dress which shapes itself over her buttocks and outlines their cleavage. Celeste extends a hand.

'Hello, I'm glad you could make it. You've already met my secretary, Ivo. Do sit down.'

Lilac sits bolt upright on a hard chair, and scans the room in amazement.

Celeste continues.

'You saw the advertisement in the *Times*, I think you said?'

'That's right. I know that it's a market research job about sex. You said the pay was two hundred per interview plus perks, and you would tell me more when I came to see you.'

Celeste leans back in the chair and swivels it round and back with a half-smile on her face. She looks rather like the tiger that Ivo fears, for she has a long, wide mouth full of small, sharp teeth. Lilac has the impression that Celeste might leap out of the chair and bite her. Instead, she leans over and hands Lilac a sheet of paper from her desk. The paper is headed, in bold, blue print 'ARDEN FOUNDATION FOR SEXUAL RESEARCH', and is subtitled, in red, 'Project Fantasy Uncover'. Below are a series of questions, with numbered codes for the replies. Lilac scans it rapidly. Her attention is held by one particular question, 'Do you ever fantasise about your penis as an object separate from you, eg a tower, a power drill, etc? (Please specify what object).' She giggles. 'I don't think I could possibly ask a man that!'

'But you have done opinion polling before?'

'Yes, but I was mainly asking people about what sort of bath salts they use, and stuff like that.'

'Well, never mind. This is a different kind of market

research. You needn't go through the questionnaire just as it's written here, as long as you find out the answers. You can fill in the codes afterwards.'

'What do you mean?'

'What I mean is that this is a practical research project. You either get the answers by asking your respondent, or else by getting him into the sort of state where he'll tell you the answers without being asked.'

Lilac looks baffled, then thinks of something which makes her smile brightly.

'You mean I have to – to go to bed with these guys?'

'No, you don't have to, but you can if you want to, and they want to. Don't forget, it's all in the cause of science, though you need not tell them that at the time. You think you could do it?'

Lilac blushes.

'Well, it would be a bit like being a prostitute, I suppose. But, you know, I've always wondered what that would be like, and thought that I'd rather like it. Well, sometimes, anyway.'

'Most of my researchers think the perks make the job worthwhile. And usually you can choose who you want to interview, and how. As long as we get a cross-section of men, some here and a few abroad, I don't care who they are. This is more of an impressionistic sample than a statistical one. But sometimes there's a man we particularly want to target. Then I choose the researcher who fancies him most, or else one who seems likely to get him to unbutton. So, how do you feel about it?'

'Okay, I'll do it. I think I'd enjoy the job. I'd like to find out more about men's fantasies too. Could be useful off the job.'

'Good, it's a deal. Ivo can give you the contract and

information pack before you leave. You'll also get a training session with Ivo and Samantha before you start. Could you come next Monday morning?'

'That would be fine.'

'What we need is a form filled in for each man you interview, and then, if you can, some sort of descriptive piece about how it was. Some researchers don't like writing it all down, but others enjoy it, I think. Do it if you can.'

The interview is at an end, and Lilac stands up. Celeste also uncurls herself to stand and shake hands. Ivo undrapes himself, gathers up some papers and follows Lilac out. His eyes drop below her waistband. Celeste stretches slowly, arms towards the ceiling. Her breasts rise and fall visibly under the ruffles. The telephone rings, and she answers. 'Arden Research Foundation.' And then 'Who told you about the project?... Oh, yes... You want to offer yourself as a subject? That can be arranged... Could you give me your number, please? One of our researchers will contact you shortly... No, there is... no payment. No, you don't get paid either... Right, thank you, goodbye.' She writes down a number, then settles herself at the desk.

Wearily, it seems, she takes another sheet from the huge pile of papers on the desk, and she reads...

3

Multiple Images

Mandy climbed the stairs of the apartment block. From time to time she had tantalising glimpses of the courtyard from the windows on each landing. A giant fig-tree grew there, surrounded by fiercely prohibitive black railings. Dark-skinned children were playing in the dust and sun down there, probably the children of the Portuguese concierge who had looked so suspiciously at her when she asked where Monsieur Deschamps lived. By the time she had reached the fifth landing, they looked like midgets. She paused to comb her hair, although, since it was a mass of wild, golden curls, it made little difference. But it was an important ritual before any such engagement. She was wearing her beige satin suit – a loose jacket, with flowing lapels and very tight trousers – and ultra-high heels. This made the ascent hard, and she silently chided Monsieur Deschamps for living in a block without an elevator. But here, in the heart of the Mairie in Paris, all the original discomforts had been preserved in the name of antiquity, and no expense spared.

Now Mandy continued to the top floor, the penthouse suite, and her heart was thumping, not because of the effort of the climb, but because she felt like that before every interview, however many she did. She reached the top, where the high, green door bore the name PIERRE DESCHAMPS in bold characters on a smart brass plate. She held her clipboard ostentatiously in front of her and was about to ring the bell when the door opened.

'I heard you coming up.'

'Yes, I'm afraid that these shoes sound like a whole battalion.'

'*Bienvenue*, Mandy. Pierre Deschamps.'

Pierre had a light, urbane voice and a warm handshake. He was tall and slim, perhaps in his early forties, with a mass of straight hair, almost the colour of honey, and streaked lighter by the sun. At first glance, Mandy hardly noticed his face, which was obscured by a pair of heavy, brown-rimmed glasses. But when she looked harder, she saw high, delicate cheekbones and bright, hazel eyes. He was dressed casually, in thin brown cords and a loose khaki shirt, elegantly cut. His whole figure and stance betokened success and ease with himself. If she was nervous, he certainly was not.

They went inside. The hall was long and painted dark red, with dim lighting from brass carriage lamps on the walls. At the end they reached a chromium spiral staircase, with light pouring down from above.

'I'm inviting you to my roof-room. You may enjoy the view.'

Mandy climbed up first, and gasped when she saw the penthouse room. Two sides were sheer glass, the third wall was a large mosaic of Botticelli's Venus, shell and all, and the fourth wall was a bank of television screens and monitors. Some of the screens replicated the views from the roof, some showed the courtyard and others showed

Mandy herself, mouth open, as she gazed round in astonishment.

'It's beautiful up here. You can see the whole of Paris.'

'Almost. I could even see the Sacré-Coeur until they put that ugly block in my way. Do you like the roof garden?'

Beyond the room was a terrace, green with palms and ferns. A small raised pond had a fountain playing in it. French doors led out to the terrace, and there were chairs and a round white table there, but the doors were closed. But still, the room felt rather like a fishbowl, with the whole of Paris and all her pigeons looking in.

'I love it! It's just wonderful! Did you design it yourself?'

'Everything here is my own design. But I am being impolite while I show off. Please sit down. I can offer you a drink, too. Muscadet and soda, perhaps, since the day is so warm?'

Mandy sat on the only seat available, a long, wide sofa, with a cover of white and green velvet in a diamond-shaped pattern. The floor, paved with Spanish tiles in the same colours and pattern, had some lambskin rugs and a few large cushions scattered about, but otherwise the room was rather bare, so that you had to look out at the view. The sofa faced a window, but if she looked to the left Mandy could see her own image look back at her from several of the screens. Pierre filled two glasses from a fridge discreetly tucked in one corner of the room and came to sit down beside her, at the other end of the sofa.

'So, your plan is to research my sexual fantasies, eh? I fear they may not be sufficiently amusing.'

Mandy sipped the wine. It was time to start, a moment she both relished and dreaded. It gave her power

32

initially, but had too often given her interviewee equal power over her. Each time was different – she would see. Certainly, Pierre was attractive and agreeable, so things might go well.

'If I could start off with some fairly basic questions? If any of them is too intrusive, please tell me.'

'It will be my pleasure. I like intrusions.'

'Are you married?'

'I was, but I am divorced now. I live – have lived – alone for five years.'

'And you work in films?'

'I'm a *metteur-en-scène* – what you call a film director. Art films, mainly.'

'Do you have a regular sexual partner currently?'

'Sometimes, but not now. I have many women, you understand.'

'Do you use the services of prostitutes at all?'

'Not since I was very young, a schoolboy, and not while I was married. And there's no need to now. This is my casting couch, you might say.' He gestured to the sofa and they both laughed. Mandy made some notes.

'Do you have a particular sexual fantasy – or maybe more than one?'

'Yes, I have one which haunts me. In effect it dominates my sexual activity.'

'Does it involve a particular person?' asked Mandy.

'No, I can imagine it with any woman,' he replied.

'Can I ask – do you have this fantasy while you are making love, or is it really when you are not, that you have it? I mean, is it a fantasy for enacting, or strictly a fantasy?'

'Both, actually. I hope this answer is not too difficult for your questionnaire?'

33

'No, that's fine. I'll ask you more about that later. Now, do you ever think or dream of your penis as some sort of object separate from yourself? You know – something like a lighthouse or a ramrod?'

Pierre laughed. He leant back on the sofa, extending his legs so that his crotch was brought into prominence. He placed his hands lazily on his thighs, one each side of the tell-tale bump. Mandy looked away demurely, and pretended to concentrate on her clipboard.

'Sometimes, I believe my penis is like an enormous sea-serpent, towing me behind it and swimming into great lakes – into your Loch Ness, maybe. And other times – yes – it feels like a great machine in some underground foundry. A hydraulic press, you know, full of power and force. Would you like to see if this is true?'

Mandy looked up again. Pierre's hands were on his flies, unbuttoning them at high speed. He was wearing the briefest of underpants, it seemed, for out sprang his cock, and stood erect. She thought he might have exaggerated the size in his fantasies, but still, this was a worthy tool, not very great in diameter, but promising in length. Uncircumcised, too, so that the foreskin hooded its delicate head and eye. Serpentine, certainly, she thought.

'Next question?' said Pierre. He had taken off his glasses as he spoke, and she could see that his eyes were large and soft, but with a challenge in them. Mandy knew the questionnaire by heart already, but she looked back at the printed sheet. Her heart had begun to beat urgently and her writing hand was shaking perceptibly as she circled a coded number. What Pierre did not know was that, as well as trying to elicit answers to its official questions, the questionnaire included space for a running commentary on the progress of the interview. So, Mandy was ringing 'Yes' and '10 minutes' in answer to the question: 'At what stage of the interview, if any, did the respondent make a sexual advance to you?' But at the same time she wondered if it was really an advance. She hoped it was, but Pierre seemed quite composed and relaxed, leaning back and drinking wine while his cock stood up proudly.

'What parts of your body particularly excite you? Do you have special, favourite erogenous zones, I mean?'

'Well, this of course.' He gestured. 'I like to stroke myself every morning here. If I am with a woman, I like her to tickle him, and to suck him very gently. And then, my nipples. I like to have them bitten, quite hard, you know.' He thought a moment. 'And my buttocks – a woman can drive me wild down there.' Mandy made a mental, as well as a written, note of all this.

'What parts of a woman's body excite you most? Do you fantasise about particular parts?'

'Of course. Like all good Frenchmen, I love especially the breasts and the arse. *C'est normal, n'est-ce pas?*'

'And fantasies?'

'Well, if I think about women, or dream about them, it is always those parts. And when I love a woman, I like her to wear something tight – like you now – so that I can see the Venus mound quite clearly. *J'adore ca.*' He stared directly at the cleft at the top of Mandy's legs. Her clipboard rested on the sofa-arm beside her and her legs, uncrossed, showed a prominent mound, and even a hint of dark showing through the light, clinging silky trousers. She shifted her legs slightly, but this only pushed up the betraying curve further.

'Would you say that you have any fetishes?'

35

'I like to see a woman naked in high-heeled shoes. Otherwise, I think not. Or rather, my fetish and fantasy are part of the same thing. I will tell you one thing I do, though, which is pure fantasy. Sometimes I go to a ladies' clothes shop, and I wait around the fitting room until the assistant who guards it goes away. Then I peep in. The room is full of mirrors and many, many young ladies are changing there. Some have nothing on but panties, some are half-dressed. I look in and I see many tits and bums, all shapes and all sizes, reflected many hundreds of times in the mirrors. This I find a tremendous stimulation – you understand? Perhaps I see you in one of these fitting rooms one day?'

Mandy recovered herself, although his gaze remained on her, and went on glibly to the next phase of questions. Usually it was hard to get through these without something happening.

'Could you tell me about your main fantasy in more detail, please?' She looked him in the eye. He extended a hand to her, and pulled her gently towards him.

'I whisper it in your ear.' He bent down and pushed back her hair, and put his mouth close to her ear. 'I like to be an auto-voyeur, you see. Shall I show you?'

She felt her heart leap, but said in a calm tone, 'I wish you would.'

The sofa stood on castors and Pierre twisted it round so that they both faced the wall of screens, and saw themselves leaning against each other, and his cock still rising between his legs. Pierre put his hand on it and frotted it slowly, with his eyes on his image. Then he turned to her and said 'Will you? Please?' Mandy's hand reached out eagerly and took the long sea-serpent, and started to work on it. Tickling, he called it, she remembered, so she used feather-light touches near the top and tremulous pinches at the root, and she felt it respond at once. A drop of clear liquid seeped from the tip and wetted her fingers, and whetted her appetite too. Pierre's eyes were fixed on the largest, central monitor, but his hand was round her shoulders, searching for a way into her jacket. The space between its large, square buttons was wide, and his slim fingers caressed her through the satin for a moment, then slipped with ease between two buttons. She wished she had not worn a bra that day, but when he found it he exclaimed 'The brassière! I adore it!', and she was glad she had. As his fingers ran round the rim of the cup, he whispered urgently to her 'I love to feel this rich fullness imprisoned in its *forteresse* and to run my fingers just inside the cup, like so, and to tease your nipple through the lace.'

As his fingers touched her nipple, she cried out softly. For her, the sensation was the same, but reversed. Her breasts felt like swelling prisoners, yearning for release by a touch or a kiss, and finally for liberation, so that they could spread and fall.

'I also like to tease your breasts as you tease my rod,' said Pierre. Her hand was still caressing him, but now he moved forward, bending over her, and undid all the buttons of her jacket, which fell away from her. As she was leaning back, her breasts were thrust upwards, and his mouth curved down towards them. The bra was oyster-coloured, made of lace and low-cut. The brown tips of her nipples were clear to see, and shaped the material's contours as they swelled beneath it. Pierre's lips were on the small, deep gap between her breasts now, and then moved round the edge of one cup, brushing the bulging flesh lightly. His tongue slid under the lace and she shuddered as it ran round the rim of one breast, slowly, and then the other, and lingered again in the crevice, then licked her again. Desperately, she wanted release, to be naked there and to see her flesh free, so that he could revel in its fullness. Pierre sensed this, and said 'I believe there are two ways to take this off. I choose this way.'

His hands were at the straps in the front now, skilfully unfastening the catches. Mandy looked at the screen opposite, and watched while he peeled down the cups, both at the same moment, so that her breasts flowed out in a liquid movement before he captured them one in each hand, and began to squeeze and compress them tenderly, moving them round so that her sense of fullness and tension became intense, almost unbearable. He bent to suck her nipples, which were hard and round as cherry-stones, and the tips tingled, while she felt his cock jerk fiercely in her hand.

'Perhaps we wear too many clothes,' he said, after some time.

'Perhaps we do,' Mandy agreed.

He kicked off his soft leather shoes and, standing up, pulled down his trousers, and took off the shirt over his head. His torso was a natural, olive colour, though not sun-tanned, and the hair curling between his legs was long and silky, the colour of honey. His prick, now deepest purple, rose out of it like the stamen of some exotic, prehistoric lily. As she sat there, bent forward slightly, it was nearly on a level with her mouth, and so, impulsively, she reached down and sucked it in, wondering at its slim hardness as her tongue wrapped round it. Then she licked it and sucked at it inside her mouth, as a child might explore a boiled candy with her tongue, and heard him groan with delight. By looking sideways, she could see Pierre's image, in profile, and herself, joined to him by her lips. But he too had his head turned to the screen, and his mouth was half open as he gasped out his pleasure.

'*Plus vite*, faster,' he muttered. But after caressing him in this way for a few minutes, slowly still, she stopped and, lowering her head further, took his balls into her mouth instead of his cock. They were taut and compact, two ripe lychees ready to burst in her mouth, she thought. She imagined that she could feel his sperm seething about inside them. She stroked them with her tongue, then nibbled them gently between her teeth. Her curly mass of hair stroked the flat of Pierre's belly as she worked at him, and gave him a warm thrill which ran back down into his loins. His hands palpated her shoulders and grasped them tightly as the frenzy rose in him, and moved to her breasts to clasp them in a grip which was almost painful.

She pulled at his balls with her mouth as if to coax the sperm out of them, and felt his organ pushing and twitching against her face, in its final throes, it seemed. So she took it back into her mouth again, and moving her head back and forth, with rapid jerks, she chewed him into a state of desperation. And suddenly, the flood broke. Her mouth was filled by three gushes of his salty spunk and he moaned and writhed above her until he had finally finished. She let go his waning cock from her mouth at last, and he sank to his knees on the floor and leant towards her, and buried his head in her lap on the sofa, still heaving.

For a while, they stayed like that. Mandy could see

Pierre's back on the monitor, and she ran her hands over his shoulder blades, which stuck out like wings from his slim, strong back. When Pierre spoke, she was surprised at the passionate anger in his voice.

'*Merdei*! I did not want to come like that!'

'What's wrong? Why not?' she asked, 'I liked it.'

'No, I had something else I wanted to do with you. My fantasy.'

'There's still time,' she said. 'You get two bites at this fantasy.'

Then he looked up at her with a mischievous smile, and said, 'You really mean it?'

'Of course I do. I want to know how your fantasy works.'

'Well, first I must undress you, completely now.'

Mandy still wore her tight trousers and shoes, although her navel in its curving setting showed over the waisband and her breasts hung free. Pierre made her stand up and opened the zip. Then he insinuated his hands inside her trousers and ran them round her belly and buttocks, as if inspecting them for size and ripeness. She felt the onset of a long, slow and growing excitement as he squeezed her buttocks. She had worn no panties on purpose, and he could reach down easily into the crack between them, which he did, touching her arsehole lightly, and then playing with it with one long finger, searching for its entrance. He prodded a little at it without entering her, then took his hands away – to her sharp disappointment – and started to peel down her clinging trousers. He bent down to unfasten her shoes, and then, finally, she was naked before his eyes and the eyes of the hidden cameras. He put her high gold shoes back on again, then turned to view her in the monitor. He appraised her slowly from her ankles up to her pubic hair, and ran his hand briefly over the slopes of her belly, and fastened them again on her breasts.

'I like a big-breasted woman,' he said. 'And most of all, with enormous brown nipples. I want to suck them like I did with my mother – to suck them hard until she gives me milk to drink.'

He stooped down and began to gnaw and pull at her breasts, while smoothing her buttocks with the palms of his hands. His eyes were shut and his face was flushed with the effort and pleasure of suckling her upstanding nipples. He pulled at one for a long time, as if to suck her dry, and then moved to the other, supporting and fondling the first with his hand. It seemed to grow until it overflowed his fingers. For Mandy, the knot of tension in her loins became a fierce, undeniable demand. She was standing so that she could see their joined images on a screen, and she found the vision turned her on even more. Her hands were running over his back and down across his bum. Remembering his liking for what she was doing there, she increased the pressure on each buttock and gave them slow, circular squeezes until she felt him gasping. The two of them stood locked in this love-knot, breathing hard and shivering as each new sensation overtook them. Then Pierre said 'And now I must fuck you – in front of the television.'

He pulled her back on to the sofa and lay beside her, on the inside, beside the sofa-back. While Mandy's face was turned towards him, he could see the largest screen beyond her cloud of hair, and he gazed at it steadily. The violin shape of her delighted him, and he kept his hands round that wasp waist which seemed to join her two halves. With easy skill, he opened her legs and pushed his own between them.

Then Mandy felt the slim rod, hard as ebony, rearing and thrusting against her belly and then digging downwards, cleaving a path through her maidenhair, grazing her clitoris lightly and forcing the outer lips of her cunt apart. Little force was needed, since they seemed to spring open at the touch of his rod. He pressed the head of his cock against her cunt-mouth for so long without penetrating her that she begged him, finally, to come into her quickly. Then, with a series of sharp half-thrusts, he entered her, stopping part-way in and then withdrawing, then repeating it, and moving in a fraction further each time. The exploratory movements, the unfulfilled promise of each thrust brought up short, soon had Mandy wailing with desire. Pierre could scarcely resist coming himself – so he slowed down his thrusts to a slow drum-beat at the very outside margin of her vagina. A warm, rosy flush was spreading across her belly with the pleasure of it.

The monitor showed two bodies rocking back and forth across the whole width of the great sofa. His head was buried in her breasts, which he continued to suck and chew. And now he drove himself into her with vigorous, deep thrusts, and speeded up the tempo of his strokes, so that she had scarcely recovered from the shock-waves of one before the pleasure of the next wafted through her nerve-ends. His hands still grasped her waist and pulled her belly against his, and her legs were clamped round him so that he could not extricate himself, even had he wanted to. Each movement made both of them gasp aloud. At last, his cock started a crescendo of violent thrusts. She was taken by surprise, the waves of pleasure drowned each other, and she screamed loudly. Just in time, for Pierre could not stem the tide a moment longer, and suddenly he poured out his spunk into her in a warm, racing current. He forced himself in again and again, then at last he lay entirely spent at her side, moaning quietly, while she tried to catch her breath, and waited for her heart and cunt to stop convulsing.

Later, they sat up and slowly began to dress. Pierre offered her more wine, and Mandy, now in her suit again, sat demurely at the other end of the sofa, and took up her notepad.

'I'm still not sure,' she said pensively, 'that I know what your special fantasy is. That was a fantastic fuck, but not in the usual sense of fantasy.'

'Can't you guess?' he asked. 'The TV screens have something to do with it.'

'Well, they act like mirrors, I suppose. But it's quite normal to enjoy screwing in front of mirrors, isn't it?'

'That depends who sees you. Perhaps I must explain. What you do not know is that in a room downstairs is another set of screens.'

'What do you mean? So what?'

'Well –' he looked embarrassed and penitent – like a little boy caught masturbating, she thought.

'Well, lying on a bed, watching these screens, is a friend of mine.'

Mandy took this on board slowly. 'Male or female?' she asked, after a minute.

'On this occasion, female. You see, I like to be watched when I am making love. A sort of reverse voyeurism, you might say. Sometimes I invite a boyfriend, and sometimes a girl. And afterwards, we talk about how it was, and maybe we try the same thing ourselves.'

'Do they generally enjoy it?'

'Why, yes. I can show you the proof.'

He went over to a panel of dials set in the side of the wall, and turned some knobs, and paused. The screens went black for a few minutes. Mandy looked out of the penthouse windows at the rooftops of Paris and the pigeons circling, and wondered whether she could ever code this experience into a series of numbers. Then, several of the screens lit up again, all showing the same thing, a large bed with a white, furry counterpane. Splayed across the bed, with her back to the camera, and her face obscured by long, dark hair, was a naked girl. She was lying watching a television set near the bed. Mandy could see, faintly, a picture of herself on the screen, standing up while Pierre bent over her to kiss her breasts. The scene went on as Mandy had remembered, but her attention wandered to the unknown girl. She was motionless for a while, then she moved her legs apart, and twisted slightly, so that the camera showed part of her belly and the wide patch of dark hair beneath. Her left hand moved down to her legs and started to work between them. Slowly and luxuriously at first, and then with mounting speed, she fingered and stroked herself there. No sound could be heard, but Mandy could see her body rocking and twisting this way and that in her pleasure, until finally she shook like a reed in the wind, rolled right over and lay still, face down on the bed.

Pierre went back to the control panel and switched of all the screen. 'Now you see – it is a very complicated fantasy that I have! When I go down later and see Annalise, perhaps we shall make love like you and I, while watching our film. Or maybe we shall watch her watching it, and masturbate each other. It is like those mirrors which are parallel and face each other. I create an infinity of images, of possibilities.'

'Is this because you're a film director?'

'No – rather I think I am a film director because I am a voyeur, and an auto-voyeur and a reverse voyeur too – or exhibitionist, if you prefer.'

Mandy wanted to go. If she stayed longer, she felt, she would want to fuck again. She was also tempted by the idea that they should join Annalise, and that the three of them should watch the film again together – an infinity of possibilities for that scenario crossed her mind. But not when on duty, she decided.

'I must go now, I have to do my paperwork, and meet a friend. Thank you for seeing me, and being so frank – and so delicious!' In a businesslike voice she added 'I'll leave you my number, so that if you think of anything else relevant to the project you can ring and let me know.'

Pierre received the coded message decorously, and sent one back.

'Yes, I will certainly ring you if I want to add another fantasy!'

4

Historical Research

It is Friday morning, and a grey, rainy one. A middle-aged man walks east down Great Russell Street towards the British Museum. He is on the portly side, but carries it off well even in the shabby brown three-piece suit, for he is a tall man, as well as a broad one. He is Hengist, a professor of Nordic History from Cambridge, and he has come up early to London to read some ancient manuscripts in the British Library. Later he plans to spend his favourite sort of weekend, sleeping at his club, playing billiards, dining with friends.

Hengist has never bothered to marry, figuring that if he wants sex he can usually get it one way or another. He has however a problem, in that he rather despises, and even hates, the animal side of himself – despite which, it is very rampant and sometimes overcomes him entirely. Actually, he has astonishing success with women, given his old-fashioned reserve and the fact that his face, if not exactly ugly, is strangely coarse. If he were a woman, the French might call him '*jolie-laide*' – both attractive and repellent. Some women, it is true, regard Hengist as just ugly, but a lot of others seem to fall at his feet. Or perhaps it is at his penis. This is rumoured to be an endowment of heroic Viking dimensions, never failing to amaze the young undergraduettes with whom he occasionally condescends to dance at the May Balls.

But today Hengist is not thinking of soft student flesh. His mind is on the Norse saga which he is about to translate, as he quickens his stride to avoid the shower which seems to pursue him along the street. Suddenly his thoughts are invaded by a remarkable pair of legs. Two-tone legs, these, striped, black on the outside, grey on the inside. Female, definitely: they are tucked into black, suede, calf-length boots. Shiny black stiletto heels, too.

Hengist studies these legs with care. He has never seen jester tights before. His eyes start at the boots, and travel steadily upwards. At the knees there is no skirt; the legs keep straight on up, broadening pleasingly at the thighs. At last they disappear behind a jacket. Just in time, thinks Hengist, who is in two minds as to whether women should be tarty or decorous. The jacket is a slightly shiny grey, peppered with black. It has astronaut shoulders, and is belted in tight at the waist. Above it, an untidy riot of tawny hair spreads out over the jacket. Altogether, thinks Hengist, this young woman bears an agreeable resemblance to an ice-cream cone.

He adjusts his pace to the legs, and strolls along comfortably behind them, mindless of the threatening cloud above him. He becomes so absorbed in his study of the neat articulation of the legs that he is almost bowled over by a taxi which swerves across him into Coptic Street. The nimble legs have gone on ahead, and disappear as Hengist is shouted at by the taxi man. Irritable now, he trudges on his way. He always resents being shouted at by the lower classes. He also resents an

47

uncomfortable stirring sensation in his trousers. He blames all this on the legs, and blames them too for disappearing. Besides, the rain has started.

The North Library of the Museum is as perennially gloomy as the main reading room, with its great blue dome, is perennially bright. The massive wooden reading tables are like snooker tables, with square brass lamps that hang over them and cast dim pools of light onto the priceless texts beneath. Unfortunately, as Celeste has discovered, certain books can only be read in this room – for example those which are indexed in the catalogue as 'PC' or 'Cup'. Celeste is starting her research into male fantasy by studying the works of the Marquis de Sade and Sacher-Masoch. Although the Museum has prodigious quantities of the works of these masters, in many and various editions, every one of them bears the shelf-mark 'PC' or 'Cup'. As she stands demurely, trying to catch the eye of the assistant, Celeste wonders idly what the letters mean. Does 'PC' mean 'Prudishly Censored' and 'Cup' stand for 'Cupidity' (arch – lust, esp. inordinate and intemperatel), she speculates. After all, the Museum people had given the same shelf-mark to her own first novel, and 'inordinate' and 'intemperate' seem to describe *Dreams of Fair Women* pretty accurately. Nice to think that one's own brain-child is to share a shelf for ever with *Juliette or Vice Amply Rewarded*, *Venus in Furs* and *The Virgin Libertine*.

'There aren't any books for Arden on the reserve shelf,' crows the brisk young assistant.

'There should be. I ordered them yesterday to be ready this morning.'

The librarian looks down again at her order slips, and leers visibly. 'Oh, you've got PC and Cup numbers. I'll have to go and unlock the cupboard.'

She takes a large key from a hook behind her desk and disappears. Sounds of padlocks being unlocked and doors creaking open. Celeste smiles to herself. So 'Cup' is 'Cupboard', after all. That makes 'PC' 'Pornography Cupboard,' no doubt. It must be a truly enormous cupboard, if it has to hold all the stuff I've seen in the catalogue.

She collects a great pile of Sadeana, and is told to sit at the table nearest to the librarian's counter. So they can keep an eye on me to make sure I'm not wanking, she thinks. The light above her place is broken, so she half-turns to her left and starts to peruse *120 days of Sodom* by borrowed light. A stack of musty leather-bound books stands on the next section of the table, but there is nobody there to read them. Probably worn himself out with so much dreary old knowledge, she thinks, and has fallen under the table. She takes up a book and starts to concentrate on the more intriguing atrocities of de Sade.

A cup of coffee and a soothing pipe in a café have put Hengist in a better frame of mind. He returns to his desk, determined to hasten through the daunting heap of books and get to his club in time for tea. He is very short-sighted, and so he puts on round, thick, rimless glasses before he settles down in front of his books. The person on his right seems to have an annoying habit of leaning towards him and breathing heavily – well, more like snorting with disgust, he notices. He moves his head round far enough to deliver a reproachful look from his right spectacle – this usually quells noisy scholars. But the breathing goes on, and his eye falls on a leg, striped black and grey, crossed over another such leg and very near his own knee. He turns away hastily, and buries his head in a good saga, feeling distinctly unsettled. Time passes.

The noise of rustling pages, a soft giggle, and the feeling of something brushing lightly against his knee, disturbs Hengist, who is pondering on the relationship between the Nordic gods Frig and Thor. He looks round again: the harlequin-legged woman is turning over pages rapidly. What are those engravings she's looking at? My God, they're all pornographic! People doing it in all sorts of positions, even in daisy-chains! Hengist stares for a moment too long, and the woman addresses him, in the requisite whisper, but still much too loud, he thinks.

'I should think that would be rather uncomfortable, wouldn't you?'

Without thinking, he replies 'the previous one looked worse to me,' and gives her a half-smile. Then he curses himself for having spoken, and still more for having been caught looking at such filth. The worst has happened now – his day is being utterly disrupted by long-legged women reading dirty books at his elbow and sniggering.

'The same engraver also did a famous sequence of Norse heroes – quite decently dressed. Would you credit it?'

The woman's voice is pleasant and cultured. Hengist cannot ignore it.

'When were they published?' he asks, with a show of interest.

'About 1780. I've got a book of them in my office actually. If you've never seen them, and are interested in that sort of thing, I could show them to you some time.'

This, to Hengist's mind, is rather forward of her, but then some scholars are surprisingly generous in the impulse to share their treasures. It's probably an innocent suggestion, anyway.

'I'd like to take you up on that one day when I have time,' he replies bluffly.

'Oh, good. I've finished here for today, so maybe you'd like to come and have lunch and see them? My office isn't far by cab.'

The woman smells of some nice, musky perfume; she also has an alluring smile, although there is a whiff of the predator in it. Oh well – Hengist is bored out of his mind with invisible rings of power and Nordic heroism, and this might be an adventure, although he usually disapproves of adventures, especially into the unknown. He soon finds himself walking through the colonnade of the Museum and introducing himself. The woman is called Celeste. She is quite masterful in the way she hails a taxi. Hengist prefers pre-feminist women himself, but decides that he can submit to this for an hour or two. Frankly, anything is better than the gloom of the North Library, even a feminist.

To say that her office was not far had been something of an exaggeration, but Celeste knew when a lie was politic. She had sensed that Hengist would be an important addition to her cross-sectional sample from the moment she caught him looking slyly down at her legs. After a twenty-minute drive, passed in civilised and erudite discussion about the monstrousness of the proposed new Library and the underpayment of academics, they arrived at her house. She took him to the ground floor entrance, this being the more respectable and imposing door; she sensed his snobbishness readily. At the front of the house on the ground floor was the 'official' office, used for meetings. It was an impersonal, white room, furnished with a large white desk and white-upholstered chairs. What was not apparent was that, at night, the concealed lighting turned it into rainbow shades. The bare walls were also useful for film projection, when Celeste wanted to run through a few blue movies.

Celeste went downstairs, leaving Hengist perched on the edge of a chair, and asked Ivo to bring up some lunch. 'Just leave it in the hall – we may be in the middle of the interview.' He looked at her darkly. Picking up the book of engravings, and a couple of other, more lubricious, volumes which caught her fancy, she returned, and Hengist spent a happy ten minutes looking at Norse heroes, all properly clad. Although he affected to be uninterested in her except as a fellow-scholar (and a rather dubious one at that, he thought), she kept noticing his sidelong glances at her legs and tits. But still, he would be a hard subject to research, she feared. She heard Ivo in the passage and went out to get the tray. Cold charcuterie, French bread and red wine was all that he had bothered to provide. Ivo could be so moody, she thought – maybe he just wasn't getting enough job-satisfaction these days.

She came back, apologising profusely for the sparseness of the lunch and complaining that you couldn't get a good domestic these days for love or money. A little unfair, maybe, but she resented Ivo's surliness. This was the sort of conversation Hengist understood, and he joined in readily. Hengist also liked food, whatever it was, and after a large plateful of salami and two generous glasses of wine, he became more expansive. He talked about Cambridge, and about his early upbringing on a country estate. He seemed to think it bad form to ask Celeste anything about herself, and yet he was clearly fascinated by her. Celeste's private diagnosis was 'Over-developed defence mechanisms; randy as a ram underneath it all.' She decided at once on the direct approach.

'I've got some etchings that might interest you in another room,' she said, and led him to the small bedroom which faced the back garden. True, there were some remarkable sketches of erotic classical subjects there. But what was most interesting about the bedroom for Hengist was that it was all in darkness, save for several peachy-toned spotlights. There were closed shutters and drawn curtains, and the spots picked out etchings of Cupid with a hand on Psyche's protuberant left breast, and Jupiter, disguised as a great swan, insinuating his neck between Leda's legs. The rest of the room was unlit, but diffused light showed a vast bed, with a pile of peach-coloured satin cushions at its head. Celeste stopped on the threshold. Hengist paused behind her. She reached out and took his hand, and led him over to look at Leda, and then at Cupid, chattering brightly about the age and style of the prints as if nothing were happening. He pressed his body close against her as she pointed out the merits of Psyche's breasts, and then said quickly, in a low voice, 'I prefer yours.'

'Oh, good. I think I prefer you to Jupiter, too.'

She turned to him and started to unbutton his waistcoat. He stood stock still, hands at his side, like a man consumed by moral anguish, until she ran her hands over his ribs, round his back, up towards his shoulders. Then, suddenly, he fell upon her, breathing hoarsely 'I want you, I want you.' He buried his lips in her hair, and pressed her to him fiercely. The man who had seemed so fusty, so stuffy, so inhibited, was transformed into a vortex of animal energy and lust. He reached up under her jacket, forced his hands between her legs and into her crotch, so roughly that she gasped, and then started tearing at her striped tights, pulling them down a short way, and then fumbling with her cunt-hair and jabbing two fingers at the margin of her clitoris, where it joined the roots of her belly.

'Quick, undo me,' he said urgently. She reached down and unbuttoned his trousers, while he rubbed his whole hand between her legs, caressing her frantically. Celeste's hand undid his fly-buttons and found its way to his cock. She felt a great mass of hard flesh, a truly mighty instrument, stoutly erect. She pulled it out, and marvelled at its size. He could not wait, but pulled her on to the bed. His trousers and shoes were still on, but his cock protruded from his flies, and he rolled on top of her, his eyes shut, and forced it into the space at the top of her thighs. The tool rammed at her tender labia, making her shiver, and then it relentlessly forced them apart and thrust itself at the door of her cunt. She was dry, for she had scarcely had time to be aroused, and she feared that he would not be able to enter her. But, so determined was the giant cock, that it battered at her gates until it found the way in. The remarkable thing about cunts is that they are able to fit any cock and grasp it snugly. Hengist's cock inside her made her feel full to the point of bursting, but it did not hurt, and it moved smoothly inside as her cunt salivated at its massive presence, and her juices started running.

After he was inside her, Hengist became a different man. He lost all inhibition and self-control; he was like a rutting boar. He rollicked in and out of her, grunted and groaned, his hands were all over her body, grasping her tits and buttocks greedily and squeezing and pummelling them. He covered her neck with kisses from his thick, wet lips, and muttered obscenities into her ear. After tumbling her for a few minutes like this, he said, hoarsely, 'Let's take our clothes off. I want to see your tits as well as feel them.' They sat up and helped each other to undress, Celeste smiling to herself as she removed Hengist's daringly red braces. Naked, he was rather too fat around the middle, but she enjoyed the feeling of his large belly pressing into hers, and he had a wonderful broad chest, matted with dark fur. He was eyeing her tits lustfully and attaching his large cushiony lips to them in an instant. But soon he wanted to be satisfied inside her.

Without any preliminaries, he pulled her under him again, and thrust his prick into her. It was easier this time, and Celeste welcomed it warmly. The size of the prick was such that she felt a delicious frisson in her anal passage as it butted against the intervening muscles, and she was almost ready to let go as the spasms of pleasure became sharp and intense. But Hengist had forgotten his partner in his own abandon. He groaned and writhed and pumped away for a few minutes, and then he accelerated the pace of his thrusts, ramming his cock into her up to the hilt each time, and shouting incoherently. Abruptly and copiously, he came inside her, sending many wild spurts into her before he had finished. Then he rolled off her and lay on his back. He was like a man whose demon has just been exorcised – entirely at peace until the incubus makes its re-entry. His eyes were shut, his big lips twisted into a tranquil smile.

Celeste, although unsatisfied, was pleased with her progress so far. But she was also strongly aroused. While

Hengist dozed for a few minutes in post-coital forgetfulness, she reached down with two fingers to her pussy and smeared some of his plentiful spunk over her clitoris. With the help of this lubricant, she soon had her own little cock darting swiftly in and out of its sheltering cover, and sending shocks of delight to the pleasure centre in her brain. She tweaked the tiny wet tip ever so gently, and sent a last urgent message upwards, and then lost herself in a series of delectable, shuddering contractions. Afterwards, she sighed with the joy of it – then she looked round and saw that Hengist's eyes were open, looking straight at her. He turned on his side, and put a large, bear-like arm round her.

'I've never seen a woman do that before,' he whispered.

'Maybe you're too keen on screwing them to give them a chance.'

'Maybe I am,' he said ruefully. 'But I do so enjoy it, don't you know. I suppose I ought to take more account of what they want.'

Celeste could see that his reserve was almost gone, and he was in a confiding mood. It might last for an hour, or only for a minute. She had to work quickly.

'I always fantasise while I'm doing it. This time I fantasised about fucking you on that table in the Library. We were invisible, so everyone else just went on reading their boring old tomes, while we were raising the roof.' Hengist looked pleased and flattered; secretly, he was thinking that feminists weren't so bad after all. Then she asked him the vital question.

'Do you have fantasies too?'

'Well, not much, not when I'm actually doing it. I'm too earthy, I suppose. I just get on with it.'

He was looking wary again. Celeste put on her sweetest smile, and kissed him warmly on the brow, then on his round cheeks.

'Oh, come on, do tell me. Everyone has some secret desires. I've got a few very odd ones myself, but I'd have to know you better before I told you those!'

Hengist had a very naughty look on his face, like a schoolboy measuring the size of his cock with a ruler behind a desk at the back of the classroom.

'Do you happen to have any satin knickerbockers around the house?'

Hengist looked embarrassed, but he also looked like a man getting something off his chest after many years. He looked expectant, too. Celeste got off the bed, and went to the chest in the darkest corner of the room. She took something out of one of the drawers.

'I bet I can guess your fantasy,' she said, smiling. Hengist burst out laughing – sounding very unpompous, and quite human for a moment. 'Bet you can't,' he said. Celeste came back to the bed, holding a large pair of satin knickerbockers, cream-coloured, with lacy edges. She held them over him, letting them graze his face and cheek, and then dangled them down his body until they rested lightly on his cock.

'Get them on,' she ordered. To her amazement, he got up obediently and started to put on the garment. She had time to notice, then, that his cock in repose was almost the same size as it was when erect. Some cocks are like that, she thought – more initial promise, but fewer surprises in store. His balls were loose and dark, and hung a long way down his thighs. Plenty of man-juice in there, thought Celeste, with a sort of relish. Hengist stood by the bed, unashamedly, wearing the panties.

57

They fitted, although they were tight across his large buttocks. (She had selected the largest pair in the drawer, women's XL size, and they were loosely cut anyway.) A snaky bump ran across them where the satin outlined and strained against his cock, and his balls dropped down visibly through one leg of the garment. Although he was altogether too stout, he looked, she thought, rather sexy standing there, the thick hair on his chest and stomach contrasting with the creamy satin texture below. She went and stood behind him, putting one hand round his buttocks. Her other hand was in front of him, down below.

'Now, just stand there and be good,' she admonished.

He was like a child in her hands, in more ways than one. As she ran her fingers lightly across the snake inside the satin, she felt it become like a hard knot of muscle. The satin was stretched to bursting point. Stroking his arse-cheeks in a slow, roundabout motion with one hand, she rubbed the other repeatedly and vigorously across the satin-clad giant, and varied the rhythm sometimes by gently pinching it from root to tip and back again. Hengist's eyes were closed once more, and he was moaning rapturously. She went on for what seemed like hours, and then decided to give him the ultimate thrill. So, squeezing his buttocks hard from behind, and grasping the whole length of his prick tightly, she moved her hand rapidly backwards and forwards. It slid freely over the soft material: beneath the satin, she felt several desperate convulsions. A deep groan from Hengist – and she sensed a wetness spreading under her hand. When she released him and looked at him from the front, she saw that his spunk-stain covered the whole front of the pants. He sank back on to the bed, and sat there with his head in his hands. His voice was husky as he said 'Thank you, that hasn't happened since I was an adolescent. I did it myself then, of course. It's much better with you.'

Celeste was picking up her clothes, scattered about the floor. After repression, desublimation, and after desublimation, reaction, she thought. She expected the violent reaction to set in soon, and wanted to be ready. She dressed quickly and went out, saying 'I'll just go and fix you a coffee. You must need something.'

Downstairs, there was no Ivo, only a note on the kitchen counter which said 'Gone out for afternoon.' No signature. What can I do about him? thought Celeste. She put the thought aside, heated up some coffee and took a cup back to the bedroom. Hengist was dressed again, and standing by one of the engravings. He affected not to notice her entrance, then turned round as if surprised to see her there at all.

'Oh, here you are. Just as well, because I really must get back to the Library now,' he said, formally and coldly.

He took the coffee and drank it standing in the middle of the room, dominating the whole space. I suppose this is how he is in his lectures, she thought, imposing and inaccessible. If only those students knew... Hengist looked into the distance, and would not meet her eye. Celeste shrugged – she could not help it if his self-dislike got misdirected at her. He finished the coffee and said brusquely: 'Must be off now, thanks for the lunch. Nice to meet you. Perhaps I'll see you in the Library again one day – but then, I almost never come to London.' They had walked to the front door. Although in a magnanimous state of mind, thanks to her recent orgasm, Celeste thought she would put in the boot, just a little. He had no right to be quite so ungracious. 'Well, I'll be there on and off, anyway. I still have to finish the research for my book on men's sexual fantasies.'

Hengist, who had gone down the steps by now, looked back at her from the pavement. His face was momentarily distorted with terror. He could not cope with the monstrous thought for long, though, so he put it aside.

'Good joke, eh?' he called, insincerely. 'Goodbye, then.' He turned on his heel, and shambled away rapidly.

'What a bastard!' said Celeste to herself, and then, 'Poor sod! Well, at least he'll be able to dream about this for years.'

5

The Initiation of Lilac

When Lilac arrived for her training session, she hardly
knew what to expect at all. She had read the material
which Ivo had given her, and knew the questionnaire by
heart. She had even practised going through it with her
boyfriend. The first problem was that she kept giggling,
especially over the question about power drills. Her
boyfriend kept interrupting the mock interview to show
her exactly what he meant, so it had taken a long time.
She suspected that most interviews would go like this,
but hadn't told him so, in case it made him jealous. Then,
to her surprise, he had asked her to write him an account
of each interview – it would be good practice for her, he
had said. At this point she began to wonder whether he
was taking pleasure in the thought that she would be the
guinea-pig for a lot of men's fantasies. She wasn't sure
whether this idea horrified her or titillated her.

She was still preoccupied with thinking about this
when she went down the steps to Celeste's office. Ivo
opened the door again, and was considerably more
welcoming than he had been on Lilac's first visit. He
even put an arm round her shoulder. He was wearing the
same black trousers as before, and a black vest, cut away

from the arms, which showed off his shoulders and biceps. For someone so slim, these were remarkably shapely and muscular. Under the vest she could see well-formed pectorals, and the tiny points of his nipples. Lilac loved his milky-pale skin, and longed to touch it, as she might a baby's cheek. It looked so soft and perfect. She followed him through the passage to a room overlooking the garden.

The room had a large bed, covered with a tasselled cloth, with Chinese embroidery all over it. There was a Japanese lacquered screen in one corner of the room, and a large wardrobe in the same style. Apart from this, there were three low, paunchy armchairs, also upholstered in a black and scarlet Chinese-style pattern, and a low, black table between them. The garden, seen through the French windows, was in sunshine, and Lilac looked out at a vista of flowering shrubs, which sheltered the privacy of the room from prying eyes. She saw a Burmese cat wander through them, then curl up in a sunny corner of the patio. Ivo told her to sit down and went away, returning with two cups of coffee. The doorbell rang and he left her alone. She busied herself by re-reading the general information about Project Fantasy Uncover. 'This research project will provide a comprehensive survey of male sexual fantasies, through extensive sampling by a team of trained researchers, using opinion poll methods and practical fieldwork. In the commentary, expert psychologists will interpret the data, and make cross-cultural comparisons wherever possible.'

The door opened and a woman came in. 'Hello, I'm Samantha,' she said, in a purring, friendly, sexy voice. Samantha was dressed like an old-fashioned schoolmistress, in a black two-piece suit, with crisp white blouse and a red, pussy-cat bow at the neck. But her face gave out a different message. She had a thick mass of streaked, blond hair, lacquered into a smooth shape swelling out from her face. Her face was heavily but beautifully made up. She was wearing thick, dark-rimmed glasses, which matched her clothes but were belied by her face. She sat down in the chair beside Lilac and started to drink the second cup of coffee.

'This is your first training session, dear, isn't it?'

'Yes,' replied Lilac nervously. 'I'm not sure what to expect.'

'Don't worry, it will be easy. I'll just show you the ropes.'

'What do you do on the research project?'

'I'm the official instructor. You see, a lot of the researchers are fairly naive, and don't know how to make up to men or get the right answers to the questions. No wonder, it's not easy to get a man to tell the truth.' She laughed loudly; Lilac smiled politely, but looked anxious. Samantha went on – 'I'm an old pro and I know how to get the best out of a man, and so I teach the girls how to get what they want.'

Lilac's big brown eyes opened wider. 'You mean, you were a prostitute?'

'Of course I was, my dear. Still am, though I do more admin these days. Same in all the professions, as soon as you get good at something, you're kicked upstairs. I'm what you would call a madam now. I've got a nice lot of girls working with me. And I do the odd bit of consultancy too – like this.'

Lilac was excited by the news. 'I've always wanted to know – what is it like?'

Samantha became very schoolmarmish. 'No time for gossip now, my dear. I'd better start teaching you how to do your stuff. You'll find out what it's like soon enough! Now, tell me, do you have a boyfriend?'

'Yes. We've been together almost five years, since I was eighteen.'

'And do you sleep with other men – or did you?'

'Well, not much – well, no, not at all, really.' Samantha looked disapproving and Lilac blushed slightly at her own innocence.

'OK, dearie, everyone has to start some time. Better sooner than later, I say, otherwise you'll think he's the only fish in the sea. Now, listen carefully.' She had brought a small briefcase, which she opened, and took out a notebook. She thumbed through the pages, studied her notes, and began to talk to Lilac as if to a roomful of students.

'Your job as a sex researcher means that you have to get information about men's fantasies. You also need, if possible, the gen on their actual sexual behaviour, and the best way to get that – and the most truthful answers you'll get – is to persuade them to have sex with you. Since you are interviewing men that you meet for the first time, in most cases, the main thing is to turn them on as fast as possible. Do you see?'

'Oh, yes,' said Lilac, trying to sound eager.

'So the first thing to do is to dress up, and wear something sexy. When you make an appointment on the phone, try to find out what sort of clothes they like, what kind of girl. Most of the researchers do that by pretending that they need to ask a few sample questions to make sure the man's suitable for interviewing. So, if he says purple stockings, thigh boots, fur, leather, or whatever it is, you try to dress like that for the interview. OK? Next thing is, you arrive at his house or a hotel, or wherever it is that you've arranged to meet. You don't know him at all. He may fancy you, but he'll be a bit suspicious, since you're after prying into his secret thoughts. So you have to disarm him, and fast!'

'How do I do that?'

'Well now, in your case, dearie, by being wide-eyed and innocent and beautiful, I should think. But the general rule is to get him talking, to put him at his ease. Admire his house or the photos of his children, or his clothes or his career, whatever seems appropriate at the time. Try to get him to talk about his life – Celeste likes to get hold of almost any info. You see, what you're doing is very much like what we tarts have to do. Men are suspicious of tarts – they think they'll take their money and short-change them, and they know the tart will see them at their most vulnerable. So, of course, we have to make them feel good, and safe. Talking is the best way to start, although sometimes you might feel the best thing is to touch them up or hug them. Sometimes we do that too.'

Lilac nodded. 'Yes, I see. I used to try and put them at their ease, somehow, even when I was only asking them about what bath salts they used.'

'The next thing is the questionnaire, if they know they're going to be interviewed. Occasionally, it's best not to tell them, but quite often they know about it and have agreed, so that's easy. As you go through the questions, they get more personal, and you'll probably find the man wants to touch you for reassurance. He's feeling sort of weak, you see, because he's telling you all his best-kept secrets. And maybe because he fancies you too. It's a very odd situation, you see, to be telling a stranger about the most private thing in your life, your sexual fantasies. So if he wants to kiss you or touch you, you must let him, and forget the questionnaire. You'll have to remember what happens after that, and take notes later – and you mustn't forget anything he says about his fantasies while he's making love to you.'

'I have a very good memory,' said Lilac, proudly.

'That's good. Now comes the difficult part. If he doesn't seem to want to make it with you, you've got to cajole him into it. Celeste thinks we get better results through practical research. And even if he is making advances to you already, you want to turn him on as much as you can, so that he's less cagey and more honest about himself, and he behaves as he'd really like to. So, I'll show you a few tricks.'

Samantha got up and went behind the screen in the corner of the room. When she came back, she was holding what seemed to Lilac like a great doll. She exclaimed with surprise when she saw that it was actually a life-size, inflatable man, complete with penis. The dummy was pink, but its body was marked out into various regions by black lines – like a butcher's diagram of the best cuts of beef – and there were red stars and black arrows painted on it here and there. Its face was crude and expressionless, but its mouth was painted as a large, circular 'Oh' of surprise.

Samantha sat the doll in her own chair, and knelt beside it. 'Suppose you're starting from cold. The first thing to do is this.' She ran the flat of her hands over the dummy's chest slowly, and round its waist, then back, rubbing its chest again. 'Men are proud of their chests – the King Kong syndrome, I call it – and although their nipples don't have the same sort of nerve-ends as ours do, they like being stroked there. Then you might try this.' She pulled the dummy forwards and put her arms round its back, burying her own head in its neck. Lilac stood up beside her to follow the lesson better, and saw that her hands were running round its rump, in a smooth, circular motion. 'You can do all this whether he's dressed or not. Some men find it more exciting when they're dressed, especially if you're naked. They know that soon you'll be undressing them, and there's a sort of feeling of safety, with danger just round the corner. Anyway, you might kiss his neck a bit, and his face too, if he enjoys that. And now, watch.'

Samantha picked up the doll and stood up with it beside her. With one arm round its waist, she started rubbing the area below its chest. Around the dummy's navel were several red stars and two black arrows pointing down in a line directed towards his loins. She stroked the region of its belly, outlined in black, with luxurious slowness, every movement taking her down further towards the dark splashes which represented the hair at its groin. Lilac was mesmerised – her own hands mimicked the movements in mid-air. Samantha's hand finally dived down and grasped the dummy's cock, and she started to frot it gently, and then with increasing vigour. Her other hand did something with a button behind its back, and suddenly the dummy cock inflated itself like a balloon and stood out horizontally. Samantha wrapped her hand round its lifelike balls, which were tight and round, and then she bent down – the top part of the doll collapsing over her shoulder – and took the cock in her mouth to tease it. After a minute, she stopped, stood up straight and flung the dummy face down over the chair back.

'Do you ever do that sort of thing with your boyfriend?'

'Well – er – not much, really. Usually he does things to me.'

'You'll find this way turns them on best. Even though they like stroking you and kissing your tits, what they really want in their heart of hearts is for you to turn them on, by main force if you like. Now, look, there are some other things which quite a lot of men like.' She knelt astride the dummy, its legs between hers, and kissed its buttocks, then inserted her middle finger, with its long, red-painted fingernail, into the gap between the buttock-cheeks, and moved it in and out. Her other hand reached through its legs, to grasp its balloon of a scrotum more firmly. As she violated the doll from behind like this, Samantha said: 'Some men come if you stick your finger up their arsehole. It's a matter of taste. The ones who are terrified of being gay hate it, but a lot of guys enjoy it without feeling it threatens their manhood. In fact, several have told me that they get the best orgasms like this, and that they dream about being shafted by a girl's fingers all the time.'

'It seems rather – naughty,' Lilac said hesitantly.

'My dear, nothing is naughty, or dirty, unless you think it is. There's nothing that's wrong in itself – it's only the attitudes that people have towards certain acts that gets them a bad name. And it's usually the people who want to do them most who are so adamant that they're wicked.'

'Yes, I see.' Lilac less doubtful now. 'But I'm not sure if I want to do that.'

'Try it on your boyfriend some time.'

'I'm not sure that he'd like it. He might disapprove of me.'

'You'll see,' said Samantha portentously. 'Now, are there any questions you'd like to ask about how to turn men on?'

'What about actually – making love, I mean?'

'You've done it before, I guess! Better remember, though, that lots of men like you to set the pace. They're tired of screwing passive wives who open their legs and shut their eyes and think of England. They want you to get on top of them, or jump on to their cocks while they're sitting in an armchair, and give them a robust fuck. Try to make the running, don't always wait. Men are like kids at heart – they want you to play with them. Most of them are an absolute pushover if you get hold of their cocks at an early stage.'

Lilac assimilated this: various expressions crossed her face – doubt, enlightenment, resolve.

'I think I can do it.'

'Good. Now you can go on to the second stage of your training. You are going to try it on the next man who walks into this room. I'll be going now. The best of luck, my dear.' Samantha gathered her notepad and bag and left the room – and left Lilac in a state of tremulous anxiety. Who would it be? What was she expected to do? She heard the front door slam – a new arrival? – and sat hunched nervously in her chair, biting her lip and waiting for the man to arrive. When the door of the room finally opened, she was somehow relieved to see that it was only Ivo. She expected him to usher someone in, or to clear away the coffee cups. Instead, he smiled at her and sat down in a chair. They looked at each other.

'Well?' he said. Lilac put two and two together, and

gulped. She searched her memory.

'Are you married?' she asked.

'Hardly! Look, it's all right, you needn't go through the interview. You're meant to be trying out seduction techniques on me. I should warn you, I'm a hard nut to crack.' He smiled wickedly, and leant back in the chair, stretching his legs out, wide apart. Lilac went over to him, after a moment's thought, and knelt on the floor beside the chair. She forgot most of Samantha's lesson in a split second, but instinct took over. She reached out a tentative hand, and smoothed back the lock of black hair which was forever falling down over Ivo's fine, pale forehead. She followed down the line of his high cheekbones with her fingers, and circled his neat chin, and stroked his neck, moving her fingers downwards and outwards to his very shoulders. He half-closed his eyes and smiled – ironically, she feared. How often had he been through all this? She leant forward and pressed her lips to his cheek, then against his lips. He responded slightly – barely – by opening his mouth a fraction. His wide, sculptured lips had a velvety softness and she enjoyed brushing and pressing hers against them. Then she ran her hands across his chest as Samantha had done, and pushed them through the wide armholes of his black clinging vest, finding those tiny, prominent nipples which had attracted her attention when he let her in. She felt a ripple of movement within him, and he stretched his legs out further. But he was playing hard to get, and now he was impassive. Her hands travelled down to the flat, taut region below the waistband of his trousers, her head bent over his chest and pushed against it, while her hands searched down below, feeling for his cock beneath the thick material. There was a shape there, but she could not take hold of it properly through the corduroy. Greatly daring, she undid his belt and zip – he closed his eyes and waited. She was kneeling between his outstretched legs now, and it was still not easy from that position to reach down inside the trousers to find his tool. Would it be as fine and pale as his face, she wondered, hoping.

'Would you like to stand up?' she asked uncertainly.

'No.' Ivo's reply was not exactly a refusal, more of a reproof. 'I mean, don't ask me if I'd like to do things. You have to make me do them, or make me want to do them.'

So Lilac took his hands in hers and gently raised him to his feet, then pulled down his trousers. He was wearing no shoes, so he stepped out of them easily. Then she could see all of him but his chest – and she wondered at the delight of his body. He had slim hips, and elongated, well-shaped legs, and tight, closed buttocks. But her eyes were drawn most of all to his cock: yes, it was pale, but no, it was not fine and thin. Instead, he had a peasant's tool of great thickness – a firm cylinder of flesh no longer than her boyfriend's but a good deal more substantial. She took it in her hand to caress, keeping the other hand behind him on his buttocks, as Samantha had, and running it down the tight seam between the cheeks. The cock weighed heavy in her hand already, and became heavier as the blood rushed in to fill out the thick cylinder. Ivo's cock inflated even faster than the dummy's and was instantly erect, not horizontal but vertical, pressing right up against his belly. She rubbed it downwards, seeing the pale foreskin draw back to reveal a gland which was flushed pure rose. Her own desire rose up and made her grasp him fiercely, while she moved

71

forward and rubbed her breasts against his chest. He let his hands rest lightly on her hips, fingers splayed out on her arse, but that was the only move he made.

Lilac had come in a soft cotton dress, gathered in at the waist, which puckered softly over her breasts. It was easy for her to reach down and take it off over her head. The camisole which she wore beneath it was on fine straps, and she let it fall from her shoulders on to the ground. Her shoes she kept on – they made her just slightly taller than Ivo. His eyes started open as she undressed and he stared at her body and fixed his eyes on her breasts. She looked like a Greek statue of Aphrodite in the buff, he thought, as he had guessed she might. He was entranced, but still he made no move.

Lilac now had the hang of this. She took him by the cock and pulled him over to the bed and sat him down. She sat herself on top of him, her legs either side of his hips and her knees bent under. One of her arms was round his shoulders, pulling him against her mountainous breasts (or so she felt them to be, beside his spare, muscular body). With her other hand, she manoeuvred his cock, forcing it down away from his belly and towards her, and she wriggled until it pressed against her pussy. She could sense that she was moist and open, and that he would fit snugly into her. But first she held the thick cylinder close against her vulva, wriggling again to get it in position. Softly, she pressed herself on to it, then retreated; then down a bit harder, so that he entered her – or rather, she took him. Another retreat, another advance and he was right inside her, filling her up completely and pressing against her clitoris with the root of his cock.

Ivo could not stop himself from sighing as Lilac

moved up and over him, and the delicious, damp friction aroused his cock to a life of its own. He could not thrust far, but he matched his movements to hers, so that he went farther inside than she intended. He could sense her excitement – she was bringing herself off by using him – and his own grew in proportion. The innocent Lilac was now having feelings she had never enjoyed before – the thrill of the chase, and the capture. She warmed to her task and pushed herself up and down on Ivo's swollen prick, each surging thrust bringing her nearer to the point of bliss. At last, he acted. He took her buttocks in his hands, delighting them with a pumping, penetrating massage. She writhed even faster, impaled on his tool in front, and captive behind in his hands – but escape was nowhere in her thoughts. As her rhythm quickened, she started to moan in time with it, and Ivo too was calling out his pleasure involuntarily. With a final, rotating thrust, Lilac made herself come, and exclaimed in surprise at the sudden, intense delight of it. Ivo had been ready to spill himself all along, and he spurted out his seed a moment after she melted and felt his pulsing cock turn to liquid inside her, while his muscles were all unstrung by the copious release.

They both fell sideways on to the bed and rested there a moment. Then Ivo said, laughing 'You'll do well. I was making it as hard as I could for you. You had to make all the running.'

'I know – and I enjoyed it,' confessed Lilac. 'My boyfriend is rather domineering, you know. I've never made love to him like that, both of us sitting on the bed. He likes to be on top of me.'

'Better not try it like this, then, or he'll get hooked on it! Let me give you a word of advice, though. Some men like to feel that they are seducing you, or that they are the ones running the show and getting most of the pleasure. You have to play it by ear. Don't just take them as you took me now, if they seem to be that type.'

Lilac was immediately anxious. 'But you thought it was all right, didn't you?'

He smiled. 'I'm a lazy sort of fellow, and I guess I'm spoilt. I just like being taken.' He ran his arms over her body and let them linger on her back, almost lovingly, she thought. 'Besides, I like you.' Lilac thrilled at the words – she was glowing with release and with her success, and felt that she might easily love, and win, Ivo. But she knew nothing about him – perhaps he was already taken by Celeste, or perhaps he was like this with all the women he initiated into this strange profession of researcher. She was wise enough to put the thought aside and still to hug the pleasure to herself.

Ivo gave her a final, friendly pat on her rump and got up, remarking that he had to go out shortly. Lilac dressed quickly, while he flexed his torso at her a little, then slipped into his vest and trousers. He went out, coming back soon with a list of addresses.

'Celeste will arrange your first two interviews, but these are some suggestions about who you should try after that. Could you ring us in a couple of weeks and let us know how it's going? Or else send in your reports, of course, when you've written them. Good luck, by the way, I'm sure you'll be a fantastic success – our star researcher! Let me know if you need any further training.' He led Lilac (who was still floating on a cloud of bliss) to the front door and courteously saw her out. Then he turned back into the house, sighing heavily, and went into the front office. Celeste was at her desk, staring hard at a book, seeming not to notice him. Ivo was doing up his trousers still as he came in.

'She'll be OK, that one,' he said.

'Good,' said Celeste grimly. 'Now perhaps you could get on with the typing, please?' There was an unfamiliar edge to her voice, which startled Ivo. He realised that he sometimes sounded like that himself. He felt a tiny surge of power inside him: to stifle it, he went over obediently and sat down at the typewriter. Celeste turned the pages of her book, but did not see the words.

6

Inside the Pleasuredrome (1)

I hate that croupier. He's going to stop the wheel at thirteen, and land me with that paunchy American businessman who's betting with gold chips. He's been eyeing me up for the last half-hour. She stubbed out her cigarette on the breasts of the mermaid ashtray and ground it slowly, watching the wheel run down and the ball trickle to a standstill.

Cy Oppenbaum Senior stared with fishy eyes from his position by the roulette table at the girl lurking behind the bead curtain. Her body was sheathed in gold lamé, curving and glittering over her Monroesque breasts, and swooping down towards her feet like a fish's tail. She was staring angrily at someone outside his field of vision, and grinding her cigarette out as if the ashtray were a face. She lifted the fluted glass – the champagne sparkled for a few seconds – then she emptied it. The wheel finally stopped, and the croupier called out '*Treize* – thirteen', and Cy stumped over triumphantly to collect his winnings. He was given a large gold token. He went over to the bead curtain and showed it to the girl. She took it ungraciously, and gestured him through the curtain and up the stairs.

Back in the main salon, customers were arriving thick and fast. There were a number of Arabs, each in a shining white burnous. There were some Sikh magnates, and a lot of prosperous-looking Americans and Australians. Girls were scattered around the great room, some chatting in groups, some sitting alone in alcoves and some seated at the bar, endlessly sipping champagne while they waited. What was distinctive was that each girl was dressed in a different colour. The tokens matched the dresses, and a man might gamble with blue, gold or any other colour, hoping to win the girl.

Juliette was wearing a silver dress, covered with small glass droplets and sequins, which threw light back at the great chandeliers. It suited her ash-blond hair admirably, and she was feeling pleased with herself. It had been a good wheeze, she thought, to get herself on the female escort list at the Pleasuredrome Casino. Rather expensive in clothes, perhaps, but she hoped Celeste would soon come through with some expenses. And she earned more than double, this way. A neat trick. Juliette enjoyed the thrill of having her subjects selected for her by chance, and besides, it saved her the trouble of recruiting them in the normal way, or picking them up at some club. She conducted her interviews unconventionally, in any case – fieldwork first and questionnaire later, if there was any need for it. She found it worked better that way.

'*Mesdames, Messieurs, faites vos jeux!*' Coloured chips clacked down on the table, and Juliette could see that there were silver chips on numbers 7, 22 and 28. The croupier was in fine form, and was fixing the wheel to give his favourite girls breaks. He didn't know Juliette yet, and so she could only hope that chance would be kind to her. And now the ball was rolling, and slowing down, and stopping at twenty-two. The croupier made a secret sign to her, looking at the alcove where she sat, finger at the side of his nose. The winner went over to the croupier and she saw him hand over a silver chip and nod in her direction. She pouted a little, then crossed the room to the table. She addressed the man. 'Would you like to follow me, please?'

She led him back across the room to another curtained door. The glass beads caught the light from the mirror ball which rotated slowly in the centre of the ceiling, and threw rainbows on her dress as she led him through. Behind was a small, spiral staircase, luxuriously carpeted in thick, maroon Axminster. This went up to the first floor, where the escorts operated. With the man following silently behind her, she went round the elliptical gallery, which looked down on to the roulette room. She reached her door and took out the key to unlock it. He was looking down at the players and was nervous, she thought. Then he turned to her and said 'I'm glad my number came up.' Juliette took him inside and locked the door again. The room was large, with high ceilings. There was a double bed and couch, an antique mahogany table with an ornate table lamp, which shed a soft light. Indian hangings were on the wall, cream, rust-coloured and black. The cocktail cabinet and fridge were discreetly housed in the bathroom, where there was also a cupboard with the kinds of accessories which escorts found useful.

'Well, I'm in your hands,' she said. 'Can I offer you something to drink?'

'Champagne's better than catpiss' he replied. 'Playing roulette I get as dry as a monk's arsehole.'

She went to the bathroom and brought back a bottle and glasses. As he raised his glass to her, he said 'Here's to twenty-two! I usually play vingt-et-un, but now, I reckon twenty-two's better. By the way, I know that your name is Juliette. They call me Jiggo.'

He was in his early sixties, she thought, and not a bad-looking man when you looked harder. His hair was grey at the temples but dark on top. He had the sort of rugged face which you associate with years spent in a hot climate; digging for oil in the Arabian desert, maybe, or running a tramp steamer in the Southern Seas. He was stocky, but not running to fat. His hands, Juliette saw, were thick and strong, hands that suggested an inner violence, when seen along with his boxer's body. His voice, too, was rough, but he spoke to her pleasantly enough.

They sat on the couch to drink the champagne. He said 'I'd like to talk a bit before we get on with it. I can't do it from cold with some bitch I don't know from the Queen of Sheba.'

'That's all right. I like to talk too. It's half the fun of this job, meeting different people. Do you come here often?'

'No, to tell the truth it's my first visit. A friend told me about the Pleasuredrome when I was still in Thailand. I've got some home leave, my first time in London in years, so I thought I'd try it. I need a woman, badly.'

'But there must be easier ways of getting one,' Juliette laughed. 'Your number might not have come up at all, all night.'

'That's the whole bloody point, don't you see? I could have gone to some cathouse, or to one of the skirts I used to know here. But I liked the idea of a flutter, getting

79

some new bird if I won.'

'What sort of women do you like?'

'Oh, all kinds. Chinese frippet's great, because they're really tight small-bore jobs. You think you'll never get your John Thomas up it, but somehow you do. Bingo. And they always love your cock, because it's so large, to them.'

'Did you go to lots of brothels when you were out East?'

'You bet I did. Several times a week. But they mainly call them massage parlours out there. The best thing I know is to have a *bekos*.'

'What's that?'

'That's when the girl gives you a massage with her body. I'll tell you about it if you like.'

'Yes, please!'

'There's a place in Pattaya, near the sea. A sort of big, square house with a courtyard in front of it, and a neon sign that flashes "THAI MASSAGE" at you. You go in and there's a room with chairs, where the punters sit around. And in the wall of the room, there's a big window, with one-way glass in it. In the room behind, there's a row of seats, bit like a cinema, with bags of crackling loafing about. You see in, you see, but they can't see out. So, they're sitting there chattering and laughing and combing the nits out of each other's hair and buffing their nails, bored to shit by the look of it. They all wear slinky black silk dresses, and each one's got a number tally. They're all fantastic-looking. Paler than you'd've thought, but lovely black hair all shiny like a gunner's boots. So, when you've had a good shufti, you choose the one you want by number and go and fork out.'

'Must be quite hard to choose?'

'That's right. The time I had my first *bekos*, I just took pot luck. Bird with dirty great pointy tits. She took me along the corridor to some kind of grot with a bath and some chairs and a massage table. First of all she undressed me – she was pretty bloody pathetic I thought at first, undoing my shoes and all that, but then I saw that she was laughing at me, teasing me all the time. As soon as we were both starkers I touched up her boobs a bit. Then she put me in the bath and washed me all over. Soap on my cock and all – I can tell you, I had a good cockstand by then, and I wanted to shaft it right up her in the bath. But she made me get out and put me onto the table. Then she gives me a right old going over – proper massage, rather tough on the old joints. Then it got really hot stuff. There was a rail above the massage pit. She held on to it with her arms, then let her body flop down all over me. She was sideways on to me, you see, and she worked her way along me, brushing me with her tits, and her belly and her twat even. Then she sort of flipped me over and started squelching her tits on my bum. After that, she pressed herself into me, pretty damn hard, up and down, and over and over again. Her cunt ponged like Chatham Dockyard when the top of her legs were over my face, but her boobs were okay when they got up against my mouth and nose. Bit like some kind of blossom you get in the Yum-yums.'

Juliette noticed that Jiggo had his hand at his flies and was undoing them. He went on. 'She was using oil too, and she'd already smothered my body with it during the massage, so we were both slippery. She slid over me like a fish. I could see that I had a great hard-on, it stuck right up between my legs. She laughed a lot at it, and rubbed her boobs across it. That sort of silky feeling all over my

81

prick was more than I could take. I came all over her boobs and her belly, and all she did was bloody giggle.' Juliette looked down again. His left hand was working busily inside his trousers, while his right held the champagne glass, and he lounged against the sofa-back as if nothing were happening.

'The best thing after that was when she called in her friend from the next door cubicle. I'd heard this girl gasping and moaning away, and I imagined that some customer was shafting her and making her come. I really wanted to see her and have a go myself. Anyway, she came in while I was still lying there, covered in oil and spunk. She was even tinier than my girl, and had very long black hair and such a pretty face that I could have taken her here and then, even though I'd just come off. I don't usually care what a woman looks like, you see, it's the cunt that counts. But she was something different.

'Then the two of them got to work on me. They turned me over on my side, and one of them lay each side of me, and then they both rubbed their boobs and legs and bellies against me, and used their hands to squeeze me and pinch me and stroke every bit of me they could get hold of. By the way, that's what they call a sandwich *bekos*.'

He stopped momentarily, distracted. Juliette could see a brown fleshy head between the fingers of his left hand. She decided to leave it a bit longer. 'What happened then?' she asked.

'Before long, I had another cockstand. The new girl was in front of me, and facing me, so I stuck my prick between her legs and she laughed as well when she felt the size of it. She had very tiny fingers, like a child's, and she ran them over my prick as it lay there. These Thais are very athletic, you know. She flipped one leg over my hips and gave me a sort of twist, and there I was inside her. What a neat, tight cunt! But I think these girls put oil inside their cunts – it felt like a warm, oily bath. And they know how to fuck – they know that a man doesn't always want to do the work. So, she screwed me by rolling her hips and body against me. And while she did that, her friend was behind me, and I could feel her little fingers working their way into my arse – right up my arsehole she went, with three fingers, it felt like. Couldn't get very far in, because her fingers weren't long enough, but she tickled the muscle there and made me open right up. What with her hand in my arse and the other one's cunt wrapped around me, it wasn't very long before I shot my load.

'They seemed to like me, though. I'd already been there more than two hours, which was all that I'd paid for. But they changed positions, and the pretty one was behind me, biting my bum with her little white teeth, while the first girl took my cock into her mouth. It was all limp and wet then, and she could just about fit it in and hold it there. She gave me a good chewing, too, and soon I got it up again. She was lying upside down, and pressing those sharp boobs of hers into my belly, and sucking and chewing at me, like I was a stick of Southend rock. Then the most amazing thing happened.'

Juliette was hypnotised by the dynamics of his erection, which was by now rearing itself up between his fingers. He saw her looking at it, and winked.

'I'll just finish the story, then we'll get down to business. I suddenly felt something forcing itself into my arsehole again. Not tiny fingers this time, but a bloody great dildo. The little witch had got some kind of vibrator and stuck it into me while I was still relaxed. My God, it felt like having the Eiffel Tower up my arse. Then she starts the machine vibrating, and I get spasms all through me. The other one's still sucking me, and I come straight down her throat. At least, that's what it felt like!'

He stood up, and started to take down his trousers without ceremony.

'See what I've got for you now.' Well, thought Juliette, it had certainly taken some time and effort to get it. She got up and slipped off her dress. Underneath, she had on a black suspender belt and silk stockings with high, gold, peep-toed shoes. 'You can keep those on if you like,' said Jiggo. When he had got out of his trousers, he bent down to unfasten her suspenders. His body, too, was brown and rugged and hairy, and his cock had the same thick, stubby workmanlike quality as his hands. He kept his shirt on, and marched her to the bed. 'Since I've won you,' he said, with another wink, 'you'd better do all the work.'

Juliette sat astride him then, and put her legs out straight forward, as if she were rowing. Her feet and shoes pressed against his head and he grasped her thighs and stroked the stockings, rolling them up and down past his cock. She opened herself as wide as she could to fit the thing in, and lowered herself on to it. The story of the Thai girls had excited her, and she could feel the moisture from her cunt dampening its lips and smearing itself on to the tip of his cock. It still took several tries to get him inside her, because her cunt-hole was small.

'You're just like a Chinese girl,' he muttered. His erection was getting thicker and stiffer too. But when she felt it sink into her, right to its roots, she put her weight on to her hands and started to move up and down. The fit between cock and cunt was so tight that she seemed to pull him with her as she moved. First, she did it with a slow, lingering motion which increased the sense of suction between them. He closed his eyes and opened his mouth, and started to breathe heavily.

Then she came down on him faster, and felt his breathing quicken. She was aroused too, and felt her heart pumping the blood down into her labia to engorge them and hold him still tighter between their cushiony pads. His hands moved from her thighs to her crotch and were caressing her there, with surprisingly delicacy and care. She felt tremors start outwards from her clitoris as he located it and tickled its tiny head with one fingertip. The friction between them increased, and she was almost jumping up and down on him as he lay stretched out beneath her. He redoubled his attentions to her clitoris – two fingers grasped it firmly between them, so that her movements had the effect of stimulating herself while urging him to a state of hoarse, panting frenzy. She felt waves of pleasure sweep through her loins and stomach as she drove herself down on him, and him into her, violently and deeply, three or four last times. Then his liquor exploded out deep into her, and he writhed and groaned like someone in an agony of release. When he was done, he twisted on one side, and came out of her at once. She felt some of his sperm, warm and viscous, come out with him and spread itself over the soft skin inside her thighs.

She lay down on the bed beside Jiggo and put an arm round his shoulders: even the toughest nuts like some creature comfort after spending themselves so completely. He grinned with his eyes tight shut, and cuddled her in his strong arms for a moment. Juliette took advantage of the moment of intimacy.

'Do you know, it's only my first night as an escort here. But I've often fantasised what it would be like, to sleep with a strange man.' White lies were, in her view, acceptable in the cause of Science.

'Christ!' His interest was aroused.

'Oh yes, I've had lots of fantasies about that, but none of them come near to the reality. It's terrific! How about you? Do you have lots of fantasies?'

'Well, if you mean sex dreams, this is one of them,' he replied.

'Tell me, what is it?'

'What I really like to do, if you want to know, is to tell a bird a good sexy story. The sort I just told you. That was true, as it happens, but I invent them too sometimes. I like to see how they take to hearing about other women, their boobs and bums. And I like to wank while I'm doing it. You see,' he added winningly 'I'm getting on a bit now, and it's not always so easy to get turned on as when I was a sproggie. I could tell you some stories about those days! My time of life, you need to rabbit on a bit first. Talk about great fucks I've known and all that. Then I get a cockstand all right like you've seen! It turns a bod on to talk about what you've done with cunt and to imagine what you might do.'

Juliette laughed and agreed. 'If I'd known, I'd have told you a few stories of my own.'

'I'm not sure that I want to hear about the great studs of the world. I was good with the one-eyed trouser-snake myself in the old days.' He sighed.

Juliette looked at her watch and said, 'But you still are. I loved it. But now it's time I went back. I've got to be on duty again.'

His eyes lit up. 'You mean, you'll go with another man again now? Randy bitch. Can't get enough, eh?' His hand strayed towards his legs, and Juliette realised that she had to do something quickly, or else be there all night.

'I have to be back at eleven o'clock, I'm afraid. House rules, you know.'

'Oh, yeah,' he said reluctantly. 'I'd better climb back into my dog-robbers, then.'

He got up and dressed with remarkable speed. An old sailor, thought Juliette, accustomed to throwing on his clothes to get on watch at a minute's notice. She dressed at a more leisurely pace. He came over and squeezed her shoulders. 'Thanks,' he whispered, 'I'll always bet on twenty-two from now on. That was fucking marvellous.'

After he had gone, Juliette washed with unusual care. Then she tidied the room and did the glasses. It only took about three minutes for her to fill in the form for Celeste. This was the boring part of the job, she always thought. Then she made sure that everything was in order for the next occupant, before going down the winding stairs to the roulette salon. There were more men there, now, including a group of youngish, loud-voiced men in tuxedos. In the blackjack room, through the high arch, she saw in the smoky, yellow-lit haze a crowd of men and women standing round the players at the table. Business here was flourishing, evidently. But blackjack was just straight gambling for money at this place, so she decided there would be no fun in watching.

7

Inside the Pleasuredrome (II)

She walked slowly across the roulette room, to give maximum exposure to her charms. She took a drink from the barman and posed against the bar, one elbow on the counter, her face turned towards the gambling table. She saw the three young men looking at her and talking among themselves, and then they engaged in whispered conversation with the croupier. He nodded. Two of them went off to the cashier and came back with a pile of silver chips, which they lined up in front of them on the table. Juliette wondered idly which one would win her, if any. Then her attention drifted away from the game, and she eavesdropped on the barman, who was talking to one of the off-duty doormen.

'So I get into the bushes by the river. It's about midnight, and no one around. I say "What about it?" and she says, "Whenever you like." Couldn't believe my luck – she was a great big woman, loads of yellow hair, nice legs. So, I'm all set to go, and I let my trousers down, and I say to her "Come on, get that skirt off if you really want it." So she drops her skirt and takes down her pants, and, blimey, she's got a dick too, would you believe it? So I says "I can't do it with you – you're the wrong sort," and she says "Oh, come on, a lot of men do it with me. I'll show you a good time." But I've got my trousers on again by now, and I say "No thanks, darling, not tonight," and I'm off like a rabbit. Pity, really, she was a nice bit of skirt, and all that long hair. Wig, I suppose.'

The doorman agreed 'Some of them TVs are the best lookers. But I wouldn't fancy one myself. Wouldn't mind knowing what they get up to, though.'

There was a loud cheer from the gaming table, and the croupier shouted '*Trois*-three.' Juliette looked over, and saw him beckon to her. One of the young men came forward and held out large silver token to her. He was tall and fair, good-looking in a very English, boyish kind of way. All right, she thought, I wouldn't mind him. She smiled at him. But then two of his friends detached themselves from the men around the table and came over to her. Both brandished large silver chips. One was dark, with dashing good looks – Italian origin, perhaps – and had a white bow-tie and white, tasselled evening scarf over his dinner-jacket. The third was thickset, more butch than either of the others, with a very short haircut and a pugilistic manner. She walked over to a more private corner of the room with them all and said, 'Which one of you first?'

They laughed, and a strong smell of brandy filled the air.

'All together,' said the butch one. Juliette was taken aback, but did not show it.

'You'd better come up then,' she said coldly, and walked off to the staircase.

She thought she could handle it, and there would certainly be something for Celeste in it. Come to that,

Celeste would owe her three lots of fees. The men, although clearly drunk, were fairly quiet now and probably far more nervous than she was. She took them into her room, and they stalked around, examining the pictures and furnishings. One of them bounced on the bed to test it. She went and found some more champagne and gave them each a glass.

'How do you want to arrange it, then?' she asked, sounding formal and businesslike. There was some snorting and giggling, then the fair man pushed the dark, dashing one forward.

'Better let Luciano go first – he needs it most!' More laughter.

'Simon can go last because he hasn't done it before. If he watches us first he'll be all right.' The butch one said this.

'All right, come on Luciano.' Juliette helped him off with his jacket. He took off his shirt and trousers himself, and stood there in his pants.

'Get on with it,' crowed the others. 'We're waiting too.'

The fair one and the butch one sat on the couch together, sticking their legs over its arms, and looked at her intently as she slipped off her dress. There were wolf-whistles as they saw her breasts emerge and hang loose and full. Luciano was more excited by her suspender belt. When he spoke, he sounded very Italian.

'Always, always,' he said, 'I want a woman with stockings and the black suspenders. Please do not take them off.'

She saw his boxer shorts distended by the stirring of his cock, and she put her arms round his bare shoulders. He was well-built and bronzed by the sun, the sort of man she would have fucked for nothing in different circumstances. She stroked his back and pressed his belly against her, so that she could feel the twitching of his prick.

'Hurry up, Luciano, I can't wait much longer,' called the butch one from the couch. She decided to shut her ears to them and fantasise that she was alone with Luciano on some sun-drenched beach on the Italian Riviera. She could probably go through with it that way. She and Luciano lay down on the bed together, and she pulled down his underpants, and put one hand on his cock, the other on his balls. He was easily excitable, and thrashed about on the bed as she tugged his awakening cock into a stiff, strong pole. He buried his head between her breasts and was nibbling the bulging flesh there and licking her nipples, and muttering *'Che bellezza! Che gloria!'* All he wanted, she could sense, was a good screw. She had her doubts about the other two, but she was determined that he should have it, and so would she. So she kept his bloated cock in one hand and pulled him against her with the other, digging her fingers deeply into the firm muscles of his buttocks, and feeling him squirm with delight as she did so. But soon he wrenched himself from her grasp and slid down the bed, kissing her belly and gently biting whatever loose folds of flesh he could gather into his mouth. She felt a pleasant tingling wherever his mouth touched. He put his lips on her pussy-fur too, and slid his tongue towards her own pink tongue of flesh buried there. She too squirmed as the two soft membranes came into electrical contact, and suddenly she wanted to have him.

'Stop hanging about, Luciano, leave that stuff to the birds,' shouted their spectators.

Luciano seemed oblivious to everything but her body. He was panting with desire, and he felt her need as well. In a lithe movement, he was on top of her, and sinking his tool between her legs and into her cunt. She was still wearing loose silk panties over her suspender belt, but the leg-holes were wide and the crotch was a mere silken string, and offered no obstacle to his searching cock.

He penetrated her as easily as a knife slips into its sheath, and the pleasure it gave her was sharp. Luciano was vigorous in his fucking of her, and he urged his cock in and out with short, rapid strokes which made her glow with pleasure and made him sweat and gasp for breath. He screwed her purposefully for some time like this, until he knew that she was fully aroused. Then he slowed down his pace to enjoy her more at his leisure, and he slithered into her like a slow-running piston into a well-greased tube, with measured, lingering strokes. This lifted her cunt to a new plane of sensation, and she felt her juice running freely, seething around his cock as he moved. He had calmed down and was relishing her as he relished any woman, and whispering the endearments that he whispered to all women. 'You are so good, so fucky! *Ti amo, carina!*'

Suddenly she felt his body lurch on top of her, and a great weight press down on her. She saw that the butch boy had launched himself on to Luciano and was riding him forwards into her, pressing his hips against Luciano's buttocks with his hands round his waist. He had reached under Lucian's body, too, and grabbed hold of his balls. He was still fully dressed. 'Ride-a-cock-horse,' he chanted. Luciano paused in his thrusting and turned his head sideways. His voice was frigid. 'If you do not get off and be quiet, I will personally kill you now.'

The weight lifted from Juliette's hips as the man got off his friend and left the bed, muttering, 'Can't take a joke, you Italians.'

Luciano turned back to her as if nothing had happened. His face was bent down to kiss her lips and her arms wrapped themselves round his waist and pulled him back on to her whenever he seemed to withdraw to the outer part of her cunt, or paused to luxuriate inside her. So, with subtle pressure she speeded up his music, although he would have liked to play the same tune forever, she thought, and she hastened him towards the climax by flexing the muscles of her cunt to squeeze him more tightly inside her. This had the effect of starting her own slowly accelerating explosion, and she cried out constantly as ten, twelve, fifteen contractions shot through her cunt and racked her whole body. Her lover wanted to go on and pleasure her again, but the desperate yearning of his cock was now beyond his control. A fierce convulsion of his balls overcame him at last and, shouting aloud, he surrendered himself to a long, wild orgasm.

He collapsed on top of her, shaking all over, and seemed to lose consciousness. Juliette lay half-underneath him. She felt comfortable and protected, and so relaxed that she was almost asleep. The other men had been quiet for some time, and she had actually forgotten that they were there, when a voice from the couch called 'Come in, sixty-nine, your time is up. Or rather, come out.'

The Italian jerked awake and rolled over beside her. He kissed her neck and breasts briefly and then said, 'I must stop now. Thank you so much. I do not stay to watch the others.' Before she could reply, he was off the bed and dressing himself. She sat up, pulling the bedspread round her shoulders. The two on the couch looked subdued, and the fair young man's face was ashen. The butch one stood up and came over to her. His voice was less rough now than she remembered, and he said, 'We've sobered up a bit now. But I'd like to screw you too – if that's all right.'

'Well, of course it is. You won me after all.'

He looked ashamed. 'We didn't quite win you fairly. Your croupier is bent.'

'I was flattered to see you all stake so much on me. Anyway, it's your turn now unless your friend wants to have a go?' She gestured to the fair young man.

'No, Simon prefers to watch. By the way, I'm Harry.' Harry started to undress as Luciano finished dressing. Juliette sat on the edge of the bed and waited, watching the two young men, so different, yet both so virile in their own ways. She wondered what time she would finally get to sleep that night. She thought she was highly-sexed, but two men in one night had satiated her appetite already. Luciano was wearing his scarf again now, and looking as cool and dashing as he had when she saw him first at the gambling table. He came over and kissed the hollow of her throat, where the two thin bones nearly met, and then her lips.

'I am going now. It is not one of my dreams to watch another make love to a woman I have just loved.'

'What do you dream of, then?' asked Juliette, recollecting her research just in time.

'Oh, me? I dream of breasts and lips and suspenders and stockings. I dream of winning a woman at cards and making love to her. I dream of fucking a woman like you once in my lifetime.' This would hardly help Celeste –

Italians were so romantic. But Luciano was already opening the door. He went out, and shut it.

Harry, naked now, came and sat on the bed beside her. He had a pale skin, and a slight fluff of hair over his chest. Younger than I imagined, thought Juliette – none of them can be much over twenty. His thick-set body would run to seed soon, she saw, but he still had some of the grace of youth about him. His cock was modestly tucked between his legs – she could see only a hint of purplish-pink there, topped with more golden fluff. She threw back the counterpane from her shoulders and looked at Harry hard, straight in the eye.

'What do you want to do with me?' she asked in a level voice. She liked him the least of the three, and she felt sure he would have some kind of unpleasant fetish. But he replied merely 'I'd like to do what Luciano did.'

'I'd better go and wash, then.'

'Oh, no, please don't do that.' He said, urgent suddenly, almost pleading. 'You see, that's what gets me going, turns me on – the thought that he's been there before. I can swim around in his spunk and feel you still warm from his fuck.' Juliette understood, suddenly. 'You're fond of Luciano, aren't you?' Harry looked pained.

'Yes, I am – but no, not like that. He's a good friend, that's all.'

You can't fuck him, so you have to fuck me after he does, thought Juliette. She said 'OK, we'll do it just the way you want it.' She started to take off her pants and her belt and stockings. Harry leant over and fondled her breasts as she did so. He had a strange way of pressing his hand against them as if to flatten their prominence, but she found it arousing. Her nipples stood out, proud and

95

pink and her breasts hung down heavily, however much he tried to erase their contours. She saw Simon hunched up in a corner of the sofa, motionless, gazing fixedly at their foreplay.

She and Harry lay down side by side. He stroked her back and rubbed his face against hers, but seemed reluctant to go further. Time was pressing and Juliette was impatient to finish. She reached between his legs and took hold of his cock. No effect. Then she took hold of his hand behind her back and shoved the fingers between her buttocks, up against her arsehole. That was it! He started violently. He relaxed as she massaged his cock to arousal, with both hands round it, running up and down the shaft, and compressing it between her fingers. Soon he was stiff, but still he seemed unable to bring himself to fuck her. So she put one leg under his and the other over his thigh, and brought the lips of her cunt up to touch the knob of his prick. She was soaking wet, with her own juice and Luciano's, and she felt Harry go rigid as his knob was bathed in their love-mixture – fear or excitement, she could not guess. She pushed her hips forward, her Venus-mound against the hair around the root of his prick, and brought him inside her. His cock felt stiff and potent, but still he seemed unsure what to do with it.

'Come on,' she whispered, 'fuck me like Luciano.' The ambiguity was deliberate. Like a spring being released, Harry was set free and suddenly his cock bounded into her, and he shifted himself to be on top of her, splaying her legs out as Luciano had done, and pressing his face and lips against her breasts. She raised her haunches a little so that he could delve into her depths, and he started a strong, fierce drumbeat inside her, which set the blood dancing in her veins. His thighs were strongly built, and his buttocks, she could feel, were a thick knot of muscle, so that when he flexed these to drive himself in, he moved with great force, and shook her whole body with each down-stroke.

After a time of fierce, almost violent fucking, he slowed down as Luciano had done, and came in with long, slow strokes. He had not the Italian's instinct for loving, and his head butted at her breasts, while his hands were clenched on her arse in a pincer grip. But she was melted again by the lingering potency of his movements inside her and more liquor coursed down her cunt-walls to ease his passage. He felt it warming his cock and was stung into greater arousal. He quickened his pace and dug into her as deep as he could go. It took only a few heaves to bring himself to the point of eruption and Juliette noticed his breathing change, and his contorted muscles relax as he let go. Another hot flood rushed up her vagina, and she felt his cock go limp inside it before he withdrew. He had made no sound, but was gasping, almost choking, and clutching her as if for dear life. Like Luciano, he was nearly unconscious after the effort and the release, and he rolled aside and lay face down.

Juliette remembered that one gambler remained to claim her. She got off the bed and went over to where Simon sat on the couch. He had finished the champagne and looked dazed and fearful.

'What about you, my darling?' she asked gently, moved by his boyish appearance but worried by his strangeness. He seemed to wake out of a dream.

'Me? Oh, hello. I don't think I'll be wanting to, but thanks very much. I'm feeling rather tired, you see.' Juliette sensed something interesting buried deep in

Simon. She put a hand on his soft, fair hair and whispered to him 'Just stay here a few minutes. I'll get rid of your friend.'

She went to the bed and shook Harry by the shoulder. He seemed to be asleep, but rolled on to his back and opened his eyes when she touched him.

'You'd better go now, I want to be alone with Simon. He doesn't want you to be here anyway, not while he's with me.'

Harry was another man now, calmer and soberer, but rather grim. He got up and dressed rapidly, while Juliette went to wash. When she came back, he was standing by the door.

'Look,' he said nervously, 'I'm sorry about all this aggravation. I put the others up to it. Don't blame them. They said it would be fun, as they'd never been in on a gang-bang before. But I don't think it was such a great idea, now.' He added politely, 'But you were awfully sporting about it. Thank you for that. Goodbye.' He left, and Juliette felt relieved. She went back and sat down by Simon.

'Are you guys all students?' she asked. He seemed more awake now, and was less pale. Obviously glad to see the back of Harry.

'I'm at University, and Luciano's doing a business course here for a year. Harry's at an army training college. He absolutely hates it. He wanted to go to University too, and couldn't get in. Bad luck on him, really, because he's a nice chap underneath it all. I knew him at school, you see.'

'Well, my darling, you're the most handsome of the lot, I think. And don't forget that you won me too. Do you want to collect your winnings?' Simon looked at her miserably.

'I've only done it once before. I don't know if it'll work again. I think my penis is too small.'

'Of course it's not. Anyone can make love – if your thing's small it doesn't matter. All depends what you do with it, doesn't it? Trying calling it your cock or your prick for a start. "Penis" is such a belittling word.' She leaned over the arm of the couch and started to take off his jacket and bow-tie. Simon did not resist, but he did not help either. He was like a rag doll, she thought. She unbuttoned his shirt and removed it, and ran her hands over his chest. He was very slight, with scarcely a muscle visible in his arms or chest, but with elegant, fragile limbs. His body was darker than his pale face, a light honey colour. Probably spends every vacation in the South of France with his rich parents, she decided.

She pulled open his trouser flies, then raised him up, so as to take down the trousers. He was still putty in her hands. She left his pants on and made him lie down with her on the bed. Then she hugged him a bit, warmly, and massaged his back and buttocks with a skilful, kneading motion that usually set men's blood coursing through their pricks when she did it. In return, he put his arms round her too, and kissed her cheek and eyes and forehead, but avoided her lips. Still shy, it seemed. She peeled off his pants, then, and slowly reached down between his thighs. She could feel his cock, still dormant, lying against a small, tight scrotum. True, his cock was not large, but she'd tried smaller and she knew it didn't matter. So she took it into one hand and began to caress it, gently at first, then with more and more pressure, rubbing from the stem to the tiny acorn that grew out of the top. She felt Simon catch his breath and move towards her. She fastened her lips on to his and at last he returned her kisses. He had a large, mobile mouth, and he encircled her lips with it and seemed to drink from them. He forced her lips apart with his tongue and slipped it between her teeth and licked inside her mouth for a time. Meanwhile, his cock became stiff in her hand and even outgrew it. She kept hold of it, though, until she judged the moment had come, when it leaped and twisted in her fingers.

She made Simon get on top of her, and locked her legs over his back and buttocks, to give him the easiest way in. He was trembling like a leaf, but eager now, and he kept his hard-on and managed to slip inside her, guided by her hand.

'Just move it about till you feel comfortable,' she said. 'And don't worry. It's not going to go away. Besides, I like your prick. It tickles my fancy – or some other bit of me!'

It was true, she had the sensation of being teased unbearably by his small, lively tool. Because it was not far inside her, it had a strong effect on her cunt-lips and even, in the position she had chosen, tickled her clit very subtly as it passed in and out. In fact, as Simon got aroused and started to move more easily within her and through the tender entrance to her cunt, she felt spurts of her own liquor coming down to swamp him, and darts of pure delight at the nerve-ends around her engorged vulva. She talked to encourage him.

'Come on, sweetie. My clit likes your cock, and see how wet I'm getting. Don't you want to drink me? Put it there, baby, and tickle my cunt-lips, while I tickle your balls.'

Simon started to fuck her in earnest, at a steady pace,

although he broke off once or twice, shuddering, as he stopped himself from coming. The more his cock teased her and plucked at her clitoris in its journey, the more Juliette herself became taut and tense, ready to spend, waiting for some stroke of release. She knew he could not last long, so she changed her position, moving her crossed legs higher up his back, raising her arse far above the bed. Now, each move that he made dragged his cock directly along the tingling shaft of her clitoris and gave her a thrill of pleasure. These piercing sensations soon came one after the other, thick and fast, until her muscles started to contract and squeeze the pleasure through her loins, and she was calling out again, loudly and helplessly. After she had enjoyed her own coming and felt warm and flushed, she reached under him to find Simon's balls, and gave them gentle squeezes of encouragement. He had gone on screwing her through-out her orgasm – heartened and excited – and he was trying to get deeper inside her than his cock was able to go, by great efforts of thrusting. But when she began to roll his balls around in her hand, their tremors went straight through his cock and he came like an earthquake, quivering, shuddering and exploding. The deluge which followed surprised even Juliette.

Later she gave him a bath and a massage, and teased his cock into action again, and made him come twice, and came again herself. He would be a good lover when he was more confident, she knew. He was glowing with pleasure at her orgasms – 'I thought I could never satisfy a woman,' he had said, wistfully – and by the time she showed him out, he seemed twice the man he had been. Juliette had another bath, and then took some more time to fill in her forms for Celeste. It was hard to know how

to classify the fantasies that had been enacted that night –
there were several strands, knotted inextricably together.
Well, let Celeste and her sexo-psychologists sort out
what it all meant. Juliette was too tired, and besides it
was four o'clock in the morning. She went to bed and
slept the sleep of the just.

8

The Round Table

The Arden Sexual Research Foundation and Operation
Fantasy Uncover are run on strictly businesslike lines.
Every month a group of researchers meets to discuss and
analyse their findings. So, on this rainy Thursday
afternoon, the white office at the front of Celeste's house
is crowded with members of her research team. Mandy is
back from Paris and wearing a new Pierre Cardin dress,
all black and white squiggles, and looking pleased with
herself, and very chic. Juliette is there too, lounging
lazily in an armchair in a loose, flowing green pant-suit
with harem trousers. Lilac has come along, although her
first research assignment has not yet taken place. Justine
is still swanning around the States and sending in long,
verbose reports which continue to infuriate Celeste. At
the table sit two other women, Cherry and Annie. Both
are smartly dressed, Cherry in a mock leopard-skin dress
and Annie in a shiny gold boiler-suit, full of zips and
pockets, tucked into high, gold boots.

Samantha comes in and says 'hello' to everyone. She
slumps heavily into an armchair and opens her briefcase.
Everyone else is rustling papers and looking through
notebooks and questionnaires.

'I had a hard night, last night,' announces Samantha. No one seems very sympathetic.

'Didn't we all?' says Cherry.

Lilac seems daunted by the gathering of star material in the room, and has been very quiet until now, but Annie turns to her and asks 'Are you new? I don't think I've seen you here before. How did you come to join?'

Lilac explains rather breathlessly adding, 'I still can't decide whether my boyfriend approves or not. He made me tell him all about the training session on Monday and then he wouldn't go to work on Tuesday. He kept me in bed all day, trying things out. I don't understand him!'

'It's very hard to understand men, but we do our best,' observed Annie.

'How did you come to join the Project?' Lilac asks.

'Well, that's a funny story. Cherry and I work together in Chelsea, you see, and share a flat. One of our customers left a newspaper behind – the *New Statesman*, I think it was. So I was flipping through it when I saw this ad saying "Sex Researchers Required". We thought it meant tarts! We rang up Celeste and she told us all about it. We thought we had the talent to do the job, and we were laughing about that. Then Cherry said, "Why don't we join in? We can spare the time. And if we meet some nice men, we might recruit a few new clients." So we signed up. It's handy, really, because we can often double up on the jobs. Celeste seems to think that's an advantage.'

Lilac takes time to absorb the full import of this. 'Oh yes, I see.' She is constantly surprised at how surprised she is – also, at how ingenious some women are.

The door opens, and Celeste comes in, followed by Ivo. Celeste looks stern, and is dressed in a tight-fitting grey suit, cut like a man's, with white shirt and striped tie. She also wears a pair of rimless, half-moon glasses which make her seem very authoritative. Ivo has a notepad and looks efficient and subservient in her wake, but he finds time to wink at Lilac. She thinks he is wonderfully cuddly in his black dungarees and the black angora sweater with the low round neck. They sit down, Celeste at the head of the table, Ivo beside her, pencil at the ready.

'First, the bad news,' says Celeste. 'I spent this morning with my accountant, going through expenses. He was very strict, too. Let me remind you what the funding for the Project includes in the way of expenses. It *does* include hotel bills where necessary, travel expenses, entertainment where justified and clothes up to a limit of £500 per person per year. It also includes stationery and phone calls. It *does not* include whips, unguents, rubber and leather goods, or silver dresses costing £900.' She looks severely at Juliette. 'The accountant also pointed out that it does not include dildoes and vibrators. He said that they count as private expenditure on leisure activity.' She pauses for this to sink in. Everyone looks down at their papers studiously.

'You must remember that we are getting public money for this research. Champagne suppers at the Ritz are not a *necessary* part of your work, are they, Cherry? Necessity is the criterion for justifiable expenditure, okay? So, watch it, all of you. Now, we have a long agenda today, so let's start. Ivo, what's the first item?'

Ivo has a typed agenda in front of him – as they all do – and is taking down minutes in shorthand. He reads from the agenda.

'Item one. Fetishes. Subitem one, flagellation and

bondage.'

'Right,' says Celeste. 'These are important fantasies for a fair number of men. Does anyone have anything to report under this item?'

More shuffling of papers.

'I had someone who wanted to tie me up with silk scarves and tickle me,' offers Mandy.

'Did he do it?'

'No, he only talked about it. He just had a thing about Liberty scarves, I think.'

Cherry speaks. 'I've got a cupboard full of whips and rods in my flat – it's in the room with the dentist's chair. One or two of my regulars are heavily into SM. I'll tell you about it if you like.' People nod and prepare to take notes.

'There's a man – he calls himself Frederick. He comes every couple of weeks on a Wednesday on the way home from work. Works in the City, I think. He always wants the same thing. First I undress him, and he puts on black rubber pants, the sort of thing you give incontinent kids. Then he gets me to tie him into the dentist's chair. It's one of those reclining jobs, so it goes back almost flat. His hands are tied down along the arm so he can reach his dick. I have to wear a bathing suit, shiny black, and boots of course. I get out an African fly-whisk and I drag it all over his body, to titillate him. Then he wants the switch, and I hit him, softly at first, and then harder, over his chest and legs and arms. He's wanking away by now and begging me to stop, even though he always tells me at the beginning never to stop when he asks me to. He calls me "Nanny" and all that sort of thing. After half-an-hour or so, I have to get out the cat-o'-nine-tails. That's a really nasty thing – made of leather and with knots in the thongs. Then I settle down to beat him hard. He comes up in red weals, and I can see it hurts him, but he doesn't seem to care. Maybe his wife doesn't see him undressed much. But he cries and snivels quite a lot – that's part of his fun. I have to abuse him too – you know the sort of thing – swear at him, insult his body, laugh at his dick. By this time it's got really big, and sticks up out of the hole in the rubber. So he brings himself off while I beat his belly. Then, if he's got the time and the money, we start all over. But this time, he gets out of the chair and takes down his trousers and I give him the cat on his arse, and stick the switch up his anus if he wants me to. Then he pays up and goes quietly. He's quite a gent, actually.'

The audience looks unimpressed. Samantha comments 'We've all had them like that, dearie. It's a bit old hat. Can't anyone do better? What about men who want to beat women?' People shake their heads. But then Mandy perks up. 'I've just had an idea. I picked up a book on the porn shelf at the airport at Roissy. It was by some guy with a foreign name, and it was a sort of fairy-story about Cinderella, and the hard time she and Buttons have being beaten as kids. Then she gets kidnapped and taken off by some baron or other and he beats her too and makes her walk about naked and lick his boots. There's lots of other stuff in it too, about people being tied up and beaten and buggered.'

'So what?' asks Juliette. 'There's plenty of that kind of filth around in the shops these days.'

'Yes, but I was thinking that if someone could interview this man, we might find out about his real-life fantasies, and that would give us some first-hand information about fladge and SM.'

Celeste has a mischievous look on her face. She speaks

with warm approval.

'That's a first-rate idea, Mandy. I think I'll take that one on myself, being a fellow-author. He uses a pseudonym, of course. His real name is Cockburn. I have read a bit of his stuff. I hear that he's someone quite respectable in everyday life. Right, that seems to tie up subitem one. What's next?'

'Subitem two. Flashers.'

'I've got something on that,' says Annie eagerly. 'I did an interview a couple of weeks ago with a car salesman. Lived down in Sussex, nice house, nice family, quite well off. He volunteered for the interview. I'm sitting there, filling in the form, and he suddenly gets up and goes to the window and unbuttons his flies and stands there waving his doodle at someone in the street. When I look out, it's a couple of teenage girls, skiving off from school, I expect. They saw him all right, and were giggling. So I ask him about that, and he says he does it quite often. I asked why he did it, whether it was a fantasy. He said yes, he had lots of dreams about it. Sometimes he'd be on stage, in a play, and he'd walk to the footlights and take down his trousers. Other times he imagines being on a balcony in a big square crowded with people who are all waiting to see him, like he was royalty, and he does it then.'

'Does he come when he's flashing?' someone asks.

'No, although he does wank himself. But he comes while he's imagining it. He doesn't know why he does it or how he wants people to react. But he told me a bit about his childhood – a big family, lots of sisters and he was the second youngest kid. I reckon he might have done it then to get attention, and maybe that's why he still does it.'

Mandy speaks. 'I've recorded an interview with a flasher, actually. He didn't know I had the recorder; it was hidden in my handbag. I've got the whole thing on tape here. Would you like to hear it?' She gets out a dictaphone-size recorder from her bag.

Celeste asks, 'Did he know you were recording him?'

'No, of course not. He wouldn't have told me anything if he'd known.'

'Give me the tape,' says Celeste grimly. Mandy is surprised, but she extracts the cassette and hands it over. Celeste addresses the women solemnly. 'There is such a thing as professional ethics, you know. We promise our subjects anonymity and we preserve it. We do not spy on them or record their voices without their consent, because that's entirely unethical. Every research establishment abides by these principles. Please don't do it again, any of you. Mandy, I'll keep this tape.'

There is silence when Celeste has finished chastising them. Then Juliette speaks up.   'Someone flashed at me the other day. I was walking to the park, past a lot of big houses, and I noticed someone in a bay window, with the net curtains drawn back. When I looked at him, I saw he was wearing pyjamas with the legs hanging round his knees. He had his hand on his cock. An elderly chap, bald, with glasses. So I did what I usually do – point at him, let my mouth hang open, then double up with laughter. He dropped the curtain. On the way back, I looked at the same window. He'd bugged me, so I thought I'd teach him a lesson. He was behind the curtain, so I stood in front of the window and pretended to make a note of his address. He pulled back the net, and I stared very hard at him and was writing nonsense on my pad – and, blow me, if he didn't just drop his trousers at me again! What can you do?'

There is general laughter, and Celeste calls the women to order. 'There's lots of data on flashers and would-be flashers in our interview reports, so I think we can move on now. Ivo?'

'Subitem three: Peeping Toms.'

'It's odd, you know,' says Celeste, 'but almost no one will admit to being a Peeping Tom. Maybe it's because it's essentially an activity of concealment. Voyeurism, the most secret of vices. Anything to report?'

'You've had my report on the French film man,' says Mandy. 'But I don't think he counts as a Peeping Tom, because everyone knew they were being watched.'

Samantha breaks in. 'I had an experience with one a few months ago. I'd gone to a cinema in the West End. It was the late afternoon performance, and not many people in the cinema. It was a long film, so I went out to the Ladies while it was still going on. The foyer was empty, no one in the Ladies either. I went into a closet and started having a piss. I heard someone come in, but thought nothing of it. Then there was a sort of scuffling noise which made me look down. The cubicle had one of those cut-away doors, ending about two feet above the ground. I bent down to see what was going on, and I saw a man's face! He was lying full-length on the floor, head near the door, looking in as I pissed, trying to get a view of my jaxy I suppose.'

'That would scare me. What did you do?' asks Lilac.

'I called out to him, through the door, "You're lucky, dearie, most men pay a lot of dough to see what you're getting a free peep at!" That fixed him. He jumped up immediately and I heard the outside door bang as he went out. That kind are all cowardice and bluster, and

110

you needn't really worry. Once they've been seen peeping, the fun goes out of it and they usually scarper.'

Celeste concludes the subject. 'It seems that it's hard to find out about Peeping Toms except through experience. But still, we'll add a new question to the interview to ask our subjects if they know anyone who's a Peeping Tom. That way, they might tell us about "a friend", and we can get some statistics.'

Everyone nods assent. 'Good idea,' says Samantha.

'Next item: item two. Gang-bangs,' says Ivo. 'Has anyone got any new data on gang-bangs?'

'You've seen my report about the Pleasuredrome,' says Juliette languidly. 'There's not much that I can add, except that it all went wrong for the boys from the start. None of them really wanted to. One just wanted a normal fuck, one was almost a virgin and the other really wanted to shaft his friend, but couldn't admit it. I wonder if any guys ever really want a gang-bang when it comes down to it.'

'I can tell you a story which proves that they do,' says Samantha. 'At least at the time. There's a certain kind of ritual about it. It happened to me once, actually. A few years back, when I was still on the game full-time, I picked up a couple of young officers from the Regiment, ar' l they visited me regularly. One evening, one of them was there, having his usual twenty quids' worth, a blow-job, and afterwards he said to me "Do you want to pick up a bit of extra next week?" "It's all grist to the mill," I said. So he told me to go down to the barracks the following Tuesday at around nine o'clock.'

'Tuesday night, I went down in my best gear. I thought something funny was going to happen, but I couldn't guess what. Johnny met me outside the gates, by the sentry-box, and took me in the side way, and down some passages into a big room. It was the Officers' mess, I think. The walls were covered with dead animals – you know the sort of thing, tigers' heads and reindeer. In the middle was a big round table. The officers were standing around beside the table, drinking scotch and smoking, and when Johnny brought me in, they all turned and cheered. Then Johnny told me to undress, so I did. I had quite a good figure in those days, and when I got my bra off they all cheered again and started to sing some song about Big-Boobed Bridget.

'Then two of the most important officers came over and took my arms. I knew they were the top brass because of all the scrambled egg on their jackets. They helped me up on to this great table, laid me down with my cunt near the table edge and my legs hanging partly over the end. They stretched my legs wide apart and two of the younger lads held them there – not that I was trying to close them! Then they all called out, "Come on, Jamie. Initiation time." There was a kerfuffle in the group and this young soldier was dragged forward by two of his mates. He was new, you see, and had to be blooded. Probably a virgin, too. He was only about twenty-two, and a pretty boy. But poor lad, he was red in the face then, and sweating like a pig. When they took down his trousers his prick was hanging down between his legs like it'd just been to a funeral. They pushed him on to the table, on top of me, and started chanting, "SHOOT A TIGER, POKE A WHORE, STICK HER TILL SHE BEGS FOR MORE" – or some such stupid thing.

'His face was just above mine. I could see that he was terrified that he wouldn't be able to perform. I

whispered, "It's all right, chummy, I'll help you a bit."
So I put my hand on his cock, where they couldn't see.
Anyway, they were all chanting away and doing a sort of
war-dance round the table. I frigged him a bit until he
was quite big, and then put him inside me. He fucked me
well enough in the end – kept it up for several minutes
before he let it all come out.

'But that wasn't the end of it. They took him away,
half-dead by the look of him, then I saw one of the top
brass standing down there between my legs, unzipping
his flies. And he got into me too, and spent himself, and
the rest of them went on chanting and shouting. Then –
would you believe it? – I was screwed by the whole
bloody officers' mess, one after another, with the colonel
looking on, and having his shot too. There must have
been twenty of them, and some of them took five or ten
minutes to bring themselves off. I was shagged out by
the time they'd all done. But still, I got more for that
night than I earned in a month. Reckon they ought to
have given me a medal too.'

Ivo has been taking notes assiduously. He looks at
Celeste now, to see her reaction.

'It's the ritual affirmation of virility, and some sort of
assertion of male solidarity against women,' she says
slowly, half to herself. 'Thank you, Samantha. That
deserves a section to itself in the final Report. It also
raises another matter which I'd put down under Any
Other Business. Perhaps we could take it now? The item
is the attitude of men towards prostitutes. You ask a few
questions which skirt around it in the interview – and
some of you ladies know what it's like from experience. If
any of you have some preliminary observations, Ivo can
make a note. Then we can see if the questionnaire needs

to be amended to get more information.'

'I've got a thing or two to say about that,' says Samantha. 'I've been on the game the longest of any of us here.' Celeste nods; she goes on.

'I thought about it a lot after that night at the barracks. Seemed to me that each soldier was excited by the fact that someone else had been in my cunt, just before he had, and that someone else's prick would be in there after his. They feel it physically, too, because your cunt's all sodden with the last one's sperm. That's one thing. Then, there's another. They didn't make me come – of course not, who could have come off at a time like that? But I moaned and groaned at the right time, and they thought I was coming over and over.'

'Yes, the idea that women's cunts are insatiable is a great turn-on – isn't it, Ivo?' says Celeste. Ivo grunts agreement, with his eyes cast down.

'And a lot of men think that the women who become prostitutes do so because they are insatiable. That's another factor in their attitude – part love, part admiration, part fear, horror and envy.'

'I think that it's the idea that they can buy you,' chimes in Annie. 'They can, of course, but they only get you for a short time. Then someone else buys you and you belong to them instead.'

'They're terribly pleased if they can satisfy you,' adds Cherry. 'But, for all they know, someone else may be able to satisfy you better. You are in a position to compare, and their wives probably aren't. So the men are imagining that you're making these comparisons all the time, and thinking their dicks are too small and all that. They feel threatened. At the same time, they want you to tell them they're the best jigger you've ever had.'

'Another thing is, some of them really want to be honest at last,' says Samantha. 'They can't talk properly to their wives or girlfriends, or use dirty words when they're screwing them. They can't be frank about sex and how they want to do it – with their wives. A tart is a pair of ears, paid to listen for an hour or two, as well as to fuck.'

Lilac's eyes are wide, wide open. Juliette is smiling patronisingly, as if she has her own superior views on the subject. Celeste says, 'The mystique of prostitutes. I'll put it on the next agenda for further discussion. Meanwhile, we'll amend the questionnaire a bit, and try to get responses. Maybe those of you on the game could think about it too. Now, item three, exotic fantasies.'

'Excuse me, Celeste,' Juliette interrupts, 'but we were talking about that item before you came in, and we didn't really know what you meant by it.'

'I'll tell you. By "exotic" I mean foreign or alien. You see, we've done a lot of research in Britain, a bit in Europe and America. But we haven't got much data on what men from other cultures have in the way of fantasy. So I just wanted to cue you a bit by mentioning it. If you can get foreigners to do interviews, or if you happen to go abroad for a holiday and can conduct some interviews, it would help immensely with cross-cultural comparisons. There might even be some extra expense money in it. But I'll give you an example of what I mean by "exotic". A couple of years ago I was in India, touring on my own. I went to Khajuraho, where they have all the erotic temples. They look like giant, ruddy-brown ant-hills from a distance. When you get closer, you see that their sides are crowded with erotic carvings, men and women doing just about everything you could imagine. The woman is upside down, standing on her hands, with her man's hands round her waist, and he's licking her pussy and she's sucking his cock. Or she has her legs wrapped round his shoulders, and her fanny's spread wide apart, and he's holding her waist and screwing her while he stands up.

'I walked round there on my own – the place was deserted. Then I saw an Indian emerging from the bushes. I feared the worst, but then I realised that he'd been reading there, because it was a shady place at that time of day. He came and chatted to me, and showed me round and explained things a bit. He was a student of history at some nearby university. He was young and very handsome, and I took an instant liking to him. I asked him whether sex in India was still the same – did people get up to all these positions nowadays? Was the *Kama Sutra* regarded as essential reading? He told me that things had gone downhill a bit since the twelfth century, and that Indians looked on these temples as vestiges of a primitive past. "But what about all these *lingams* and *yonis*?" I asked. "I've seen those phallus statues in the doorways of temples, with the *sadhus* pouring oil on them to anoint the *lingams*."

'Well, he thought all of that was purely symbolic nowadays. So I asked him about his own sex life and whether he had great erotic fantasies, inspired by all this phallus-worship. He said his best fantasy was a sort of dream he had recurrently, where he became the god Siva, and had a huge great prick. Siva is the Creator and the Destroyer. Ramesh – that was his name – dreamt about having twenty arms, wielding axes and cymbals and lotus-flowers, and going round having the pick of all the girls in his village, because it would be a religious rite and a great blessing if he deigned to fuck them!'

Celeste stops and everyone is silent, although Ivo is still taking her words down in shorthand.

'Actually,' she continues, 'he took me back to his room and re-enacted his Siva dream, which was rather a good turn-on, as it turned out. Anyway, that's what I mean by exotic fantasies – anything outside our own culture, which you can find out about. See if you can meet some men from the Far East, or Africa, for example. Right, then, what's next, Ivo?'

'Item four: recruitment.'

'Yes. I think we need more team members. You're all on your backs all night, if you'll pardon the expression. So I'm taking on two more. Lilac is one of them. The other is a man.' A frisson of interest runs through her bored colleagues.

'He almost convinced me that I'd be prosecuted for sex discrimination if I didn't give him a chance. He also said that he'd get more out of man-to-man discussions with some blokes than a girl can. We'll see if he's right. Anyway, you're not likely to meet him. The other thing is that we need some help to interpret these results. I'm looking for a professional sexologist. When I've found one, I'll get him along as a consultant.'

'I think we really want some expert advice,' agrees Samantha. 'We know a lot about what men do, but we don't know why they do it.'

'Last item: hardware demonstration,' says Ivo who is in a hurry to end the meeting for some reason. Celeste reaches into a box which she brought in with her and opens it and pulls out a large purple object, shaped like a phallus, but with lots of small bumps down its shaft, and with two small horns on its knob.

'This is a new vibrator from the Sexofab chain. They've sent it to the Foundation for testing and approval.'

The object is handed round among the women and they examine it with care.

'I think the horns would get in the way,' someone says.

'What are all those bumps for?' asks someone else.

'To increase friction, I suppose. But they're too close together. What you need is just one or two near the root.'

Someone turns the power on and the phallus shudders and twitches in her hands. 'Wrong speed,' she comments. 'It's only got one speed and that would be too fast.' She touches another switch and the object rises and falls in her hands. 'That's better – it saves you doing all the work yourself.'

'It's too big to go in a man's arsehole,' says Cherry.

'Depends on the arsehole,' says Annie.

'Does anyone want to take it and test it?'

Annie volunteers.

'That seems to conclude the agenda, unless there's AOB,' says Celeste.

No one speaks up.

'All right. Good luck with the assignments. See you all next month.'

She gets up and stalks out, followed by Ivo, who has picked up Mandy's tape from the table and put it in his pocket. The girls now relax a bit, and yawn and stretch.

'She's in a foul temper,' laughs Juliette. 'Bet she's not getting enough these days. But Ivo looks knackered.'

'Come on, no gossiping about Celeste,' says Cherry. 'We've got a meeting of PUSSY in half an hour. That reminds me, would anyone like to join PUSSY?'

'What is "PUSSY"?' asks Lilac.

'It's the pros' union. Looks after us and gives legal advice and does a good job on public relations for tarts. Annie and me and Samantha all belong. We're thinking of setting up a branch at the Foundation, though Celeste won't like it. A salaried staff branch. Would any of you like to join?'

'I'm not sure. I don't think my boyfriend would like to think of me as a prostitute,' stutters Lilac.

'You know I shan't,' Juliette says. 'I'm too busy working for that kind of thing.'

'Anyway,' Mandy adds, 'we're sex researchers. We should join the research technician branch of ASTMS or something like that.'

'Suit yourselves. You may think you're a cut above us, but we're all the same under our skirts. Anyway, we've got to go. Come on, Annie.' Cherry gets up and leaves, followed by Annie and Samantha. The others linger, chatting, for a while, then let themselves out since no one is about.

In his bedroom on the floor above, Ivo is listening to Mandy's tape. The flasher describes how he's done it in front of the Royal family, in front of vicars, at political meetings and outside the door of the House of Lords. He is a dedicated flasher, who believes that his cock is an ornament to mankind, and that no one should be deprived of a sight of it. Ivo has the volume turned up too loud. It attracts Celeste's attention, and she gets out of her bath and goes along the passage. She listens at the door. An unfamiliar, metallic voice is talking. 'So, just as the Lord Mayor's carriage was approaching, I jumped up and held on to the lamp-post with one hand, and got out my prick with the other, and waved it right at him. That time, I got fourteen days . . .' Celeste flings open the door suddenly, and sees Ivo naked on the bed, his flies wide open, his hand at his crotch.

'You're too impressionable, that's your trouble,' she snorts, and leaves the room, slamming the door.

9

Judicial Adventures

The reason why Celeste was bathing at three in the afternoon was that she had to go to Cambridge later. Her old College had the convivial habit of asking former students to go and dine with the dons at High Table once in a while. Only the alumnae who had made good were asked, and this was Celeste's first invitation, although she had graduated more than a decade previously. Clearly, some don had heard of the Arden Foundation and had judged her to be a person of sufficient importance to grace the institution. Since she was curious to find out more about College life as viewed from the top, Celeste had accepted.

At King's Cross, she selected a book from the thriving pornography section of the station newsagent. It was Cockburn's latest fairy-tale, about the babes in the wood. She spent a disagreeable hour skimming through it on the train. There was a lot about young people hanging upside down from hooks in the ceiling and having their arses violated. The instruments were various everyday items of kitchen equipment, wielded with fiendish glee by teams of middle-aged men in drag. Celeste hoped the young ones were over the age of consent, although she reflected that their consent would spoil the entire point of this sad stuff which was that the victims were defenceless and unconsenting. She couldn't see how anyone would be turned on by it all – if a literary scholar of the future did a word-check on it, the most frequently occurring words, the keywords, would be found to be PAIN, SHAME, TEARS, ARSEHOLE and HUMILI-ATION. But he was clearly rather clever in titillating his readers by tuning in to all those childhood stories, so as to exploit their built-in sexual symbolism and innuendo.

At Cambridge, she took a cab out to her old College. The women's colleges had been built some way out of town, perhaps to avoid contamination by male students. Her College was called St Kitty's, but known throughout the student population as St Pussy's. Arriving at the Gothic pile, with its forbidding gatehouse, her heart sank as it always had when she came back at the beginning of term. In those days, she had been locked in at night, to her intense frustration, but now at least she could decently escape by ten o'clock. After making one short detour she went across the court to the room suggestively called the Senior Combination Room. A number of hoary old female dons were there, many of whose faces she remembered, including those of the lesbian couple, one an expert on Sapphic poetry, the other a Shakespeare specialist who had maintained at length, and defiant of ridicule, that Shakespeare was a woman.

Celeste was welcomed by her old tutor, and introduced to various people. Those who recalled her, or pretended to, also pretended that she had not changed a jot in fifteen years. If only you knew, she thought. The only thing in College which had changed at all, she concluded, was that it had a few male dons now, having recently gone co-ed.

Otherwise, the sherry was just as vile and the heavily Victorian decor just as tasteless as ever.

Celeste met the new College Principal, a manful sort of woman. So old Ratbag must have retired. She also met Herr Doktor Müller, a Visiting Fellow from Germany, and was introduced to a judge. This cheered her up, since she planned some future research into the judiciary. She noticed that many of the dons were now younger than she was; this depressed her. A gong struck in the distance, then it was time to file up the stairs to Hall. The familiar smell of boiled cauliflower evoked some nostalgia, but not much. At dinner, she sat between Doktor Müller and a young man, the new Eng Lit don, who specialised in post-post-structuralism; and opposite her old tutor and one of the lesbians. Conversation turned to her work. She admitted to the young man that she had written fiction. 'Arden? Oh, *Arden*,' he said. 'Just remind me of the name of your last book. Your third, wasn't it?' Actually, it had been her first, but she didn't disabuse him.

On being told the title, he said, 'Ah, yes. I felt that it was ripe for a post-structuralist analysis. It was the silences, the spaces, the lacunae, rather than what you actually wrote, which stimulated my interest most.'

Celeste considered replying that most people found that it was the words between the spaces which stimulated them best, but she let it drop, since he had obviously never read a word of it. Then her old tutor wanted to know the plot, which was tricky. It's rather like the Abbey of Thélème in Rabelais's *Gargantua and Pantagruel*, a sort of house full of women, where everything is possible – very picaresque, she told her. This seemed to satisfy that inquisitor. But the lesbian was persistent, and wanted to know what the women did

123

there, and whether men were allowed in. 'I'll send you a copy,' said Celeste. This shut her up. However she did not add that she had slipped into the Library on her way over and had deposited two copies of *Dreams of Fair Women* there, one in English Literature, one in the French Culture section.

Herr Müller, by contrast, was interested in the Arden Foundation. When she told him, in the most discreet terms she could devise, about Project Fantasy Uncover, he brightened up considerably and said that he was a psycho-sexologist himself. His questions about her work became so pressing that she decided the best way to change the subject (since his voice was very loud) was to invite him to visit her in London. She would show him her Archive and the Foundation Museum. That would be his pleasure, he said, he would certainly come. Celeste drained a glass of very fine Tokay. So that's what they spend the money on from the Scholarships they abolished, she thought.

By this time, they had chewed their way through the well-remembered lemon and rubber-meringue pie, and they rose from the table. The students stood up as usual, and Celeste noticed with pleasure that mini-skirts were back, in a big way. Under the crow-like black gowns, several dozen pairs of thighs flashed at her – some silver, some purple and some gold. She also noticed a number of male students. 'So, you've finally admitted some men?' she asked the lesbian. 'No, we haven't,' she replied grimly. 'At least, I haven't.'

The dons left the dais and wound their way down a spiral staircase into a small, panelled room, where decanters of port winked in the candlelight on a highly polished table and silver épergnes of fruit were dotted

124

about. This time, Celeste was seated next to the judge. His name, Grackle, was familiar, and she seemed to recollect reading about him in the gutter press, which purported to admire his relentless persecution and punishment of the sort of sex crimes which sold them several million copies each Sunday. Mr Justice Grackle was being lionised by the dons present, because he was rather grand and might become a benefactor of the College, since his daughter was a student there. He was used to this, and was holding forth with court anecdotes.

When she could get his attention for a moment, Celeste asked what he thought about the laws on prostitution. 'Honoured in the breach,' he said, and laughed loudly. He was visibly irritated when she pressed him for a serious answer, levity being the order of the day on such occasions, but he eventually came up with the proposal that prostitutes should be outlawed entirely, and punished by imprisonment if they persisted.

'That's interesting,' said Celeste, innocently. 'Because I've got a research project on hand about men's sexual fantasies and I think most of them would be impossible if tarts didn't exist.' The judge prudently decided to turn his attention elsewhere at this moment, so Celeste was left to talk about recent developments in microchip technology to the Fellow in Electronic Engineering opposite her – a very sexy redhead with saucy eyes. Celeste thought she would make an excellent researcher, concentrating on the Hardware Design and Application section of the project. Soon the party broke up and people started drifting off, rather the worse for wear. The judge offered her a lift back to London. This seemed like the ideal opportunity for an impromptu interview, so she accepted.

He was a large, stately man, with a great mane of grizzled hair, steely grey eyes and a smooth, pink face. His mouth had a vicious twist to it, and she could imagine him donning his black cap with relish to pass sentence, had capital punishment not been abolished. He was wealthy enough to afford a Mercedes, anyway. Celeste strapped herself in, and they set off for London.

Unknown to Celeste, Judge Grackle had a small cottage a short way off the motorway, which he used for weekending; his wife didn't know either, and she hardly noticed whether he was home at weekends anyway. So Celeste was surprised when he drove up a slip-road and plunged them into a dark, unknown tract of countryside. They had been talking amicably enough about the proposed new divorce laws, and she was waiting to introduce a few of the standard questions in the hope of conducting the interview.

'Are you married – and where are we going now?' she asked, squeaking slightly.

'No, I'm certainly not married. I thought I'd take you to my little cottage for a cup of coffee, just to break the journey.'

After a few minutes, he turned into a drive through some tall trees and stopped outside a small, thatched cottage.

'Reminds me of Hansel and Gretel,' she said, thinking of Cockburn.

'Ah, yes. But, my dear, you are the witch,' he said gallantly, opening the front door. He took her arm and led her through a door, then switched on a table lamp. The room looked banal enough, except that it had no chairs. There was an old fireplace, a large table and a big old cupboard built beside the chimney with a padlock on the

126

handle. In front of the fireplace, which had a gas fire in it, was a large, furry white carpet. The judge lit the fire and went out. He was back a minute later with a decanter of port and two glasses. 'I'm out of coffee, I'm afraid,' he explained, and poured out the port. He gave her a glass and looked at her, but in an odd way. Then he spoke in a kind of chant:

'Do you solemnly swear that you will never reveal
    and ever conceal
All that you may touch taste see or feel
At this special court of the Central Circuit?'

'I do,' said Celeste with mock solemnity.

'Then drink, and no heeltaps.' She obeyed, draining the port in one gulp.

Mr Justice Grackle reached over with a refill. 'How much do you want?' he asked.

'Thank you, that's quite enough,' said Celeste, with her eyes on the brimming glass.

'I don't mean port. How much do you want?'

Celeste's mind worked quickly. She wondered why on earth he should have taken her for a tart. She was dressed with rare decorum, in a loosely knitted dress. True, her tits did push through it a bit, but that was quite common with knitted dresses. Maybe he'd misunderstood her reference to Project Fantasy Uncover. But still, here was a chance to get an insight into judicial low-life. She was always telling her researchers to take any window of opportunity – now she must practise what she preached.

'A hundred pounds.'

'Good God. When I was your age my clerk sent me out at half the price.' He still had his keys in his hand, and he went over and unlocked the cupboard in the corner. Inside was a jumble of garments and some shelves.

127

Celeste could not see much of its contents in the dim light. He got out some old black rag and threw it across to her. 'Put it on – after you've undressed.'

Celeste undressed quickly, standing by the fire. The judge watched dispassionately as she peeled off her dress, up over her waist and her head. She wore no bra, and her breasts swung down voluptuously from her collar bone, and curved up temptingly from her rib cage. Where the two axes met were pouting pink tips with nipples flushed deeper pink. She was wearing frilled, oyster-grey panties, quite loose, and she just stepped out of these. All that remained were her tights and high-heeled shoes.

'That's enough,' he said. 'Put on the robes.'

She picked up the black garment, and found that it was a sort of gown, similar to the one she had worn as a student, but far longer. She struggled into it as he watched. Then he reached into the cupboard and came out with an old, grey barrister's wig.

'This too, if you please,' he said. When her costume was complete, he came over and ran his hands about her body, pausing at her navel to wriggle his little finger inside it, then raising them to cup her tits tightly and palpate them forcefully. He didn't seem to appreciate her body much, she thought. Grackle by name and Grapple by nature.

'Now help me to undress.' She still couldn't fathom what he wanted, but at least she knew how to do this, and soon the judge was naked down to his socks. To jazz up the proceedings a bit, Celeste handed back his waistcoat and said 'Put this on again, please. I'm a waistcoast fetishist myself.' He made a face somewhere between a grin and a snarl, but put the waistcoat on.

'I'm glad that women have their little whimsies too.

Now – take my cock in your right hand.' The judge's dongle, like his face, was pink and shiny and thick, and was lying peaceably between his legs as if all this drama had passed it by entirely. Celeste knelt down and put a hand on it, and began to dandle it gently. 'Not like that – much harder. Try to squeeze out my spunk.' She obliged, and clenched the instrument tightly, in both hands now, and abraded it mightily up and down. After a time, during which he stood rigidly above her, and seemed scarcely to breathe, she felt it take an interest, and begin to come to life in her hands. He had no foreskin, so the knob stood out firmly, becoming a deep, stormy purple as the shaft rippled through her fingers. Her shoulder was up against his leg and she felt him start to shake.

'Enough, stop, quickly, I don't want to spend out here,' he said urgently, and got down on his knees beside her. She was encumbered by the tangled arms of the gown, but he pulled it open and made her lie down on the white rug. She still held his cock tight, and could feel the quick pulses beat through it.

He reached out for his trousers, which lay on the floor nearby, and took out a pair of nail-scissors. Celeste feared that he was going to shear or damage her pussy-fur.

'No thanks,' she said. 'I can get all the topiary I want at my hairdresser's.'

'I won't hurt you – it's just a fancy of mine. I like to do things the hard way,' he said. He put his hand between her legs and pulled the tights away from her crotch, then cut a small hole in them. Then he flopped down on top of her and she felt his hands pushing his cock, now rock-hard and exigent, through the hole, and assaulting her cunt with it. The lips were still sealed and he rammed himself against them, using his hands to add force and direction. Finally, they parted and his cock-knob battered at the soft flesh which lay warm and moist inside, then circled and fumbled until it found the entrance to her cunt.

'Nice pussy,' he said, but without any real enthusiasm, as he dug right into her with one long, fierce shove. She felt him relax when he had reached his goal, and the tip of his prick – which was long now, as well as thick – seemed to knock at the head of her womb. She relaxed too, because now she knew she could manage him, and the tiny salivating centres near her cervix sent a welcoming spurt of dewy juice, despite herself, to quench his cock's thirst. The judge was fit and vigorous – and heavy too. He ground Celeste's backbone against the floor as he splayed himself across her to get further inside, and rocked on his knees. His head was crushed against her neck, and he was biting her there, quite hard, and sucking the soft skin of her throat. The surrounding tights held his cock prisoner and guided him straight to the heart of her, so he could not deviate in his onward rush nor rub against her clitoris. Even so, his excitement infected Celeste instinctively, for he was like a rutting boar, snorting and snuffling, and she felt herself breathing faster, but still without altogether losing control, as the head of his cock slammed against the tender, unseen nerve-ends in the walls of her cunt.

His urgency diminished after a time, and he slowed his pace, but redoubled his force. She felt a long pause, followed by a sledge-hammer blow into her vital self, which shook through her belly and thumped against her heart. Then another pause, while her cunt seemed to hold its breath, anticipating the next infringement of its privacy. So stiff had he become that he was soon withdrawing entirely, then rushing into her from a distance, like a man running to throw a ball with extra speed. He laced his hands under her and round her buttocks with an iron grip, to pull her against him and impale her further. It was as if he wanted to drive right through her and come out the other side. She decided to make him come quickly and completely, so as to exhaust his supplies. So she rested a hand on his arse, and parted its padded cheeks with a long, sharp middle finger. The next time he drove into her cunt, she rammed her finger up his arsehole with equal ferocity.

'No, don't, stop it!' he shouted, then she felt his anus twitch and almost swallow her finger, and he screamed and came like a geyser, and the hot spunk went everywhere – inside her and out, over her thighs and buttocks. He lay still on top of her, crushing her completely as his limbs relaxed, so she rolled him off and left him on the floor, and went over to the table to drink some of the port. Not her favourite drink, but she thought she'd earned it.

The judge was snoring softly, and she reckoned it would be a few minutes before he woke. She took off the wig which was hot and itchy – she decided never to be a barrister, whatever betide – but she wrapped the robe around her and went off to explore the cottage. The kitchen was neat and bare, a bachelor's kitchen with little more than a sink, a kettle and a microwave. Going upstairs, she turned left and found herself facing a door which carried a brass nameplate in ornate Victorian style. 'MENS REA', it read, which meant nothing to Celeste. She went in, and saw that this was in fact the bathroom. There was an old-fashioned, round-backed wooden chair with arms, with a strange round hole in the seat; there was also a great carved mirror on the wall, and a very long, wide bath. He must sit in the bath and preen himself. Apart from that, she noticed only one odd thing in the room, which was a large circular plate of brass, propped up against the wall. She did not stop to examine it. The bedroom, on the other side of the staircase was as bare, hygienic and uninviting as the kitchen, with a double bed and a wardrobe and little more. On the bed lay a single paperback. *Coming To Terms With Sex*, the title read. She tried the wardrobe door, but that was locked. Grackle had obviously intended to come to the cottage after Cambridge – Celeste was maybe just the icing on the cake – because the heating was on everywhere. But the whole place gave Celeste a chill feeling.

She heard the judge's voice – 'Are you there, young woman? Are you there?' – and went downstairs again. He was sitting on the rug by the fire with the jacket round his shoulders, and drinking the port. He looked less grim and punitive and seemed more friendly. Orgasms work wonders, even on judges.

'I thought you had run away, like Hansel tried to. I'm sorry if I was a bit rough with you just now. But it's – it's been a long time . . .'

'That's all right, it's a professional hazard. Most guys come to us in the same state.' Celeste had decided to maintain her camouflage. Even if Grackle wanted to imprison tarts because he needed them, he would probably look more kindly on Celeste the prostitute than on Celeste the sexual investigator. He beckoned her to join him by the mean little gas fire, and then he looked at her tentatively.

'Another hundred pounds for another hour? After that, I'll drive you straight back to London.'

'All right, one more hour. But only if you'll tell me

something. What is it you've got about wigs and robes? Don't you leave your work behind you even when you're with a tart? Most people do!'

The judge was going to say that it was none of her business, but then decided he had better humour her, since there was something he wanted her to do. She read this in his changing expressions.

'It's not easy to explain. Sometimes I put on my wig and robes myself, and have the girl screw me in them. It depends how the mood takes me.'

'But the gown gets in the way of fucking and the wig is awful, it's so scratchy and musty. So why do you do it?'

'Well, really, I think it's a way of cocking a snook at my colleagues, and maybe at myself. As you might guess, it somehow debases my profession when I roger a tart dressed in the symbols of our authority. By demeaning my profession I demean myself – just as I do when I'm with a prostitute.'

The frankness of his reply surprised her, but he had had a lot of port.

'Gosh, that is complicated.' She was playing the innocent. 'Why not leave the whole thing out and have a straightforward fuck?'

'Because that's what turns me on.' This conversation ran the risk of becoming circular, so Celeste tried another tack. 'What else turns you on? Do tell me – we've got another fifty minutes, after all.'

'Clockwatcher!' It was the first joke she'd heard him make and a good sign, she hoped. 'I'll tell you – I'll show you – if you promise that you're unshockable,' he said.

'Yes, I'm unshockable. But there are some things I won't do because – well, because I don't think tarts ought to be degraded,' Celeste replied firmly.

133

'It's quite all right. You won't have to do anything – or not very much. I need a helper, or an observer. Come up to the bathroom.'

No robes this time. They went upstairs together. He went over to the circular piece of brass, picked it up and put it down on the seat of the wooden chair. It dropped into place snugly. Then Celeste noticed with foreboding, and interest, that towards the back of the brass plate was an upright protrusion, a cylindrical brass tube tapering to a rounded end. It was two inches long, maybe, and about an inch in diameter at the bottom, less at the top. She had an intuition about what would happen next.

'Come and help me,' he said, and went over and placed himself above the chair, as if to sit down. She took hold of his arms, ran her hands up them, then down over his hairy waistcoat to reach beneath his hams. 'Guide me,' he ordered, lowering his buttocks. She pulled the cheeks apart, distending his vent with her fingertips to coax it onto the up-thrusting spike. Though she could not see what she was doing from where she stood in front of him, the cold brass found its own way between her fingers and into his yielding, pulpy orifice. He was used to this self-imposed penance, and wriggled as he settled into the chair, to fit himself completely over his toy. His body stiffened and shook as it penetrated him, then he sank on to the seat.

'To horse! To horse!' he urged. She scrambled up to ride him, sticking her legs between the chair-rails at the side, and pushed down on him, in a cantering rhythm. He put his hands on her head and pulled her towards him, then clapped them round her hips and dragged her further on to him. Lucky that her legs were long – she could rest her feet on the floor and use them as a support when she moved on top of him.

The judge's eyes were shut, and she could watch his face. Rapture and anguish alternated there. The brass tube must be right up inside his arse now, she thought, as she jigged up and down on his lap. He rose and fell slightly in the chair by flexing his own legs, and he began to pant and moan.

'There's a key at the side – turn it.' She fumbled around the chair and found a sort of butterfly nut, and turned it. 'Not that way, the other way,' he said angrily. As she turned it in the other direction, she felt his cock bound and press against her, sandwiched between her belly and his paunch. She realised that the tube was adjustable; by turning the nut she was forcing it further up into his back passage. As it got longer – and, no doubt, wider at the bottom – she could sense its progress through the forbidden channel by the swelling rigidity of his prick and by the man's accelerating, rapid gasping. 'Jump on me, drive me on to it.' Celeste fairly shot up and down, almost galloping on top of him, and she heard him groan and felt him shake as the delight of the intrusion racked him, and the lengthening, thickening tube stretched his arse-muscle and burrowed still further into the passage. She gave the nut another twist – it would turn no more. She slid her hand between her body and his and grabbed his cock, starting to wank it with brutal speed, while she went on bouncing her body against his. He could not last long, she judged, and she felt a foretaste of his joy, a small warm trickle from the knob of his cock. He began to shift himself up and down in the seat as fast as he could, then he gave a rending cry and started to shout, almost a bark, as the spunk leapt out of his cock and sprayed his waistcoat and her tits and belly.

He subsided slowly, leaning forward against her. After a time, he said 'Turn the key the other way.' So she did. She felt his body relax, and then a final long shudder as the cylinder was retracted entirely through the chair-seat and his aching, stretched muscle contracted again in a last orgasmic spasm.

'Would you care to go downstairs and dress?' he said. 'I'll join you in a minute.'

Celeste was sitting by the fire, warming herself with some more port, when he came in, looking very pale, and shivering. He put on his clothes quickly, and drained his glass. He looked at her calculatingly.

'Would you take a cheque?' he asked. That's an old trick, thought Celeste.

Aloud, she said 'Why, certainly. I'll probably frame it and hang it on my wall, since I'm not so short of money.' He thought the better of it and searched his pockets, and found a thick wad of twenty-pound notes. He peeled off ten, then added another, saying 'I'm obliged. You would do pretty well at the Bar.'

'Perhaps you'll remember that the next time one of us comes up in front of you.'

The journey home took another forty minutes, but Mr Justice Grackle was too tired to talk, so Celeste lost the opportunity of further research into judicial practices. But she felt that she had done well, in the circumstances. When she arrived home, Ivo was still out, even though it was two-thirty in the morning. Celeste thought for a moment that she could use some of the Judge's money to rent herself another young man, and with this thought she fell asleep, her face buried in Ivo's pyjamas.

10

Voodoo and Vortex

Dear Celeste,

This is an astonishing place, it just oozes excitement and sex. It's changed a bit since the old days – there's still a streetcar, but nowadays you go to 'Desire' by bus. I never quite made it. And black women don't drive mule carts up the street singing out 'Crawfish, crawfish' like they did in *King Creole*. The tourists have taken it over, but the old houses in the French quarter are still there, with their high balconies propped up on iron stilts, and people drink Hurricane cocktails on them at Happy Hour. The inhabitants are mainly Catholics, very observant, and there's a Saint's Day parade most weeks, for some Saint or other. I stumbled on one when I arrived, and walked through the procession. There were girls on floats, dressed in green, sequin bathing costumes, with white mink stoles round their shoulders, and guys dressed like cavaliers on horseback, some with the sequinned girls up behind them, long hair tumbling down behind. Further up the parade there were mule carriages, the sort tourists usually get ripped off in, occupied by the local Mafiosi – lots of middle-aged and old men, very fat and smug-looking, with tuxedos and bow-ties. No doubt the girls in mink were their daughters, and their fathers had paid a fortune to get them the chance to expose their tits all round town.

When I arrived in Nawlins, as they call it, I booked into a hotel in Rue Royale, one of the old ones with a big courtyard behind. They wanted to put me in the old slave quarters at the bottom of the well of the courtyard, but it was very dim and sunless down there, so I paid extra for a room at the top, with its own balcony. It seemed a better place for entertaining, and I could sit out on the balcony and study the local talent. I slept most of the next day – jet lag and the day with Robert finally got to me. But in the evening I went down Bourbon Street, the red-light part of the old town. There are places with live sex shows, and to attract the punters they have photos of them in the windows, naked girls in twos and threes, and even heaped up in pyramids. Some have tassels on their tits and feathers in their crotches. But the photographers have the odd habit of putting a square of black ink over the girls' pussy-hair in these photos – like our newspapers do on the faces of someone who's been arrested but not charged. Maybe men recognise girls by their pussy-hair in these parts. As I walked along there were neon signs flashing GIRLSGIRLSGIRLS at me, and loud music coming out of the clubs. The men around changed, like werewolves, at twilight. When I started it was still daylight, and no one bothered me, but as soon as dusk fell they came out of the woodwork – black guys and white guys – and made passes at me as I walked along. I can't think why, because I was only wearing my old jeans and a tight black bolero, cut-away round the waist. It was too hot to wear more anyway, because the climate here is like a Turkish bath most of the time.

I heard some jazz drifting down from Conti Street, so I walked towards it. At the crossroads there was a band of black musicians playing to a crowd. They knew all the old tunes and were going through the full routine, playing some funeral dirges and marching up and down in slow time. Their music had a rough, raunchy sound and the crowd loved it. All the players were young – college kids, maybe? I was fascinated by the one playing the sax; he was twenty-five, perhaps, and very slim, with a remarkable face – high cheekbones, big, sculptured lips and flaring nostrils. Then they played an old song called 'Wild About That Thing', all jazzed up. I thought I noticed the saxophonist catching my eye once or twice as they played it. Then there was a pause and he came round with the hat. He was wearing white trousers and a T-shirt which clung to his chest in the heat. I put in my dollar and listened until I got hungry, then went off to eat some Cajun jumbo shrimps at Arnaud's.

Someone had left a fold of matches on the restaurant table and I looked at it. It was black with silver print and said 'LIVE NETWORK FOR MEN! Hot Talk! LOTS OF ACTION! Not a recording!' I took it back to the hotel. Although I was tired, I rang the number, hoping the hotel receptionist wouldn't listen in. A very soft Creole voice answered and said 'Hello, I'm Gloria.' I couldn't answer, because she'd know I wasn't a man, so I just breathed heavily. Gloria is probably used to heavy breathers and doesn't care, since they've already paid their two dollars for the call. She started to talk.

'My skin is light brown, and I have black hair down to my ass, and my boobs hang down halfway to my waist. I'm putting my hands on them now and they feel real good, like very ripe water-melons. Down below I'm kind of furry and my clit sticks out like a tongue, so I can just see it peeping through the fuzz. I'm going to put my fingers on it now. I wonder what your prick is like? I like them hard and horny. Gee, I really love a man who can stick it right up inside me and screw me until I beg for more! I wish your prick was right here now because my cunt is opening up and I can get two of my fingers inside it easy, and the juice is really running out. (Noises off; door slamming).

'Here's my buddy Charmaine and she's come along to visit with me and enjoy. She's wearing a cute little red G-string and not much else. She has long blond hair and tiny boobs with little, pointy tips.' Another voice came on the line: 'Gloria is licking my nipples now and she's driving me crazy with that hard pink tongue of hers. When she sucks the left one and bites the very tip, I get so wild that she has to put her hand down on to my pussy and run her finger along the clit. She's licked her finger, so it's good and wet down there, and I can feel that I'm going to come if she does that much longer and now she's put her mouth there and her tongue is tickling me and licking the shaft of my clit and OH,OH,OH,OH . . .' The line clicked and was dead. I suppose I'd had my two dollars' worth. After that I stayed awake for a long while, playing with myself and I came two or three times before I fell asleep.

The following day, I walked out and looked in the shops. The Marie Laveau shop was full of spells and aphrodisiacs and magic which could take away hexes and potions for getting your lover back if he left you. Voodoo is still a big scene round here. I rode a streetcar to the zoo and watched a hippo trying to mount his mate without success, and I relaxed in a warm bath when I came back. In the evening, I queued to get into Preservation Hall, along with hundreds of other tourists. The place was packed by the time I got in and I was standing near the back when someone said in my ear 'I see you in the street yes'day. How y'all doin'?' It was the street musician I had noticed before. We stood together and listened to the music for a time: it's amazing how old a lot of these trumpeters are, yet they play like angels. Then the musician said 'They ain't got no liquor here – let's go get ourselves a drink.' We went to Pat O'Brien's and we sat out in the courtyard with the fountain lit up in rainbow colours and Scott, as he was called, got me a Margarita. We talked about music because he knows all about black jazz. His favourite singer is Bessie Smith and he told me that some of her songs were real hot digadoos if you listen good. I said I'd like to hear some.

Scott isn't actually a professional – he works in a bank downtown, but he loves playing for fun. While we talked, I was thinking what a good subject he'd be for the Project because he was so full of life, and the way he moved his hands and body was very sexy. I didn't have to recruit him because he suddenly said 'Y'all want to come back to my place? I can play you Bessie Smith and cook some blacken' redfish too, if you want.' We walked to his place and went upstairs. The flat was near the market and the river – you could actually see the Mississippi glimmering down below in the moonlight. Scott had one big room with a bed, a tall black shiny music centre with winking green lights, an old HMV with a great golden sound trumpet, green and purple jelly bags, and feathery pictures strung from the ceiling on long strings which twisted and untwisted in the faint evening breeze. The walls of the room were smothered in posters for jazz festivals, and pictures of his favourite singers. Next door was a tiny kitchen. He got out some cold beer and lit some candles and came to sit beside me on the bed as we drank.

'I was thinking, maybe it's not blacken' redfish that you need. Maybe you want some jelly-roll?'

'That sounds nice,' I said. 'Have you got some in the fridge?'

I couldn't think why he laughed so much, doubling up. 'I ain't keep'n jelly-roll in the freezer, honey,' he said, and squeezed my shoulder. 'I'll show you what I mean.' He put on a record – Bessie Smith was singing and it was called 'Kitchen Man'. The words were rather mysterious and hard to hear, but then Scott said 'Listen now' and I heard *His jelly-roll's so nice and hot, Never fails to hit the spot, I can't live without my kitchen man.'*

'Now can you guess where I keep my jelly-roll?' asked Scott. I could, of course.

'Do you want me to give you some? I sure like to.' He came over to me and put his arms round me, and rubbed his cheeks against mine. He had strong black arms and the muscles in them were bulging, but he was gentle, and pressed his hot lips all over my face, almost dreamily, before I kissed him back. I began to feel a quivering down in my cock-house, and I knew he was turning me on.

'It's so damn hot, I figure I'll take off my pants,' he said. He took off all his clothes while I watched, so that I could see his shapely, sexy chest with all the muscles and veins standing out, and his long limbs and flat belly, and high, tight arse, all glistening in the candlelight. He stood there like a statue, in profile – he must have guessed what

142

a turn-on it is for a woman just to look at him. I couldn't see his cock, which hung between his legs, but I was desperate to touch it.

'Y'all want to take off yo' rags? We have real steamy weather in this town.' I followed his example: he didn't help me undress, but stood quietly and watched. Then he said 'I guess we'd both feel good after a shower,' and led me off to his bathroom. After Robert, I realised that all Americans think of showers as an integral part of their sex-life, and here was more proof. The bathroom was white and small, and the shower was a tiny triangular corner of it, hardly big enough for one person. 'Go ahead,' Scott said. So I showered while he watched me without touching me, and I felt tingling and nervous and aroused, just feeling the water on my tits and looking at him and knowing what was going to happen.

He gave me a big red towel and then said 'Now watch this.' He got in and sprayed the water all over his body, and then turned the nozzle downwards so that it played right on to his cock, not in droplets, but like the stream from a hose. I saw him shudder all over, and then his cock came into sight. It just rose up, without him touching it at all, until it pointed outwards like a warning finger. Then he made it twitch, and it waved about, getting thicker and higher all the time. He laughed while he did it, and called out to me 'See where I store my jelly-roll. Y'all want some now?' I was hungry for this delicacy by then. But he stayed in the shower a bit longer, teasing himself until his prick was at its full length – some length! – and rubbing the water over his shoulders and chest. 'It's far out, this water on my jelly-roll,' he said 'it makes me dance and sing.' He didn't dry himself but came and took me in his arms, and I could feel the steamy wetness rising from his skin in the hot little room, and his cock was standing out against me, prodding at my belly and making something inside me lurch towards him. He kissed my lips then, enfolding them in his and making a vacuum which drew my tongue out until it touched his sharp teeth.

We went back to the room by the river and lay down on the bed. Every nerve in my body was pricking and tingling because of the shower and because my lust was sharper with every minute that he held me and touched me. Bessie Smith was still singing the blues... *'got me goin', he's got me goin', but I don't know where I headin' for.'* But I knew where his cock was heading as I felt it press on my half-closed thighs and squirm between them and make towards my vulva. He was lying partly on top of me, raised up on an elbow, and his head was bent over mine. He kissed my hair and forehead and then nibbled and licked at my ear-lobes, while my mouth pressed against his chest and I explored his prominent pectorals and the tight, hard buttons of his nipples with my tongue, letting it salivate over them and leave a snail's trail as it passed. He eased the ripe acorn of his prick between the folds of my pussy and let it rest, quite stationary, at the soft oozing mouth which led into me. Electric charges shot through me where our soft membranes touched and I felt him growing tense as a coiled spring. But still he did not move. Instead he said 'I don't believe in getting to first base before the ball's been thrown.' The music echoed his words: *'Whoa, Tillie, take yo' time, you got all night to do that thing.'*

I was more impatient, and I reached down and fastened on his cock. It filled my hand and stretched out beyond my fingers, and I felt the blood surging through it. His balls beneath were round and yielding and slightly furry. I pulled him against the rosebud opening of my cunt and edged the knob inside, experiencing a wave of wild sensation. Then he moved into me of his own accord, and at last the whole length of his prick lay drowsily inside me, as if resting again. 'Sweet mama, I love yo' sugar-bowl,' he crooned, and laughed. 'Let me stir it with my spoon.' He moved as if his prick were paddling in my cunt – advancing a little, then retreating as the waves came to wash it. I lost all sense of my body and became one great, raw nerve, which every movement tantalised and swamped with sensation. I begged him to fuck me faster. Then he embedded his delectable jelly-roll in me with heavy strokes, and I was shouting out nonsense and wrapping my arms round him to bring our bodies close, to merge them together. I don't know whether I came or not because those moments were one long ecstasy. He was still controlled, though breathing fast and laughing for pleasure as he ploughed me. But after some time he withdrew. I said 'please don't stop!' and he said, 'Don't worry, honey, I'll be back to press your button soon.'

He stood up and reached under the bed and brought out something – a mask – which he put on. Not one of the carnival masks that all the tourist shops in New Orleans sell, but a real, fierce, witch-doctor mask, striped black and white, with brown owl's feathers spattered over it. He was transformed into a dangerous beast, dark-bodied and sharp-toothed. But I saw him laugh as his eyes flashed out at me through the holes.

'Y'all not about to leave Nawlins without seeing some Voodoo magic?'

'No, I suppose not. Where is it?'

'This is the Voodoo, I'm the magic!'

'Say that again!'

He bent over the bed and pressed the mask against my face till it tickled and I sneezed. With his face hidden and his prick rising like the sun, he seemed more potent, a phallic symbol made flesh. For a moment I dared not touch him in case he jinxed me.

'When I eat his doughnut, All I leave is the hole,

Any time he want to, he can use my sugar-bowl' sang Bessie.

The moment of fear and awe passed, the words of the song infected me, and I reached forward with my mouth to where he stood and took his prick in. I guzzled his jelly-roll, sucking and licking and chewing it every which way, while above me he jittered and danced at the end of it like a bear on a rope tugged by its master. He called out endearments mixed with obscenities and dipped his cock right into my mouth as he moved.

Again, suddenly, he withdrew. He tore off the mask and flung himself down on the bed, seizing me in his arms and rolling us both over and over until he was on top again. Breathless and laughing, he said 'I not stall'n any more. Give me all yo' honey now.' His cock flew towards my cunt and swam in, so wet were the lips and the passage inside. He plunged in and out like someone possessed – maybe the mask had bewitched him too.

'... easy, honey, don't get rough, of you I can't get enough,

You make my love come down...'

We thrashed about together, rocking and rolling, joined at the loins for ever, it seemed. We gasped and moaned in unison – with each deep, penetrating twist of his magic instrument he evoked a musical note from me, and he sang too as his cock buried itself in my cave time and time again. We reached a crescendo, a fierce allegro of thrusts, and a whirlpool of aching pleasure sucked me down into my chasm and drowned me there, and I was shouting and crying, while he let himself go in a thundering spasm and filled my quivering cunt with a foaming deluge.

We spent the rest of that night together and the next day I left the hotel and moved in with him for the week. We went on the paddle-boat 'Natchez' and danced to jazz as she steamed down the great river, and drank at the Old Absinthe House and we fucked every day, nearly all day. At the weekend he borrowed a boat and sailed me up a bayou on the Lake, where we screwed each other senseless while the water slapped on the mud outside and the wild parrots screamed blasphemies at the alligators.

I can't describe everything that happened and anyway, Celeste, all you want to hear about is fantasy, not real life. It wasn't much good for the Project, I'm afraid, because I think Scott was a man who had no fantasies or perversions or fetishes. He had dreams, though, and he liked laughing at the sun in my hair and seeing what I was like in a boat and telling me how much he loved my tits and, above all, just fucking me in all sorts of places and positions. Anyway, it's rather painful to write about it because I fell in love, but I had to leave him to go on to Phoenix. So I'll just stop writing about Scott, and tell you what happened in Arizona.

Dear Celeste,

I'm just about to fly to Mexico now, so I'll bring you up to date before I go. I'm writing you a letter instead of a report, because I can't do all those forms. Arizona is full of phallic symbols, especially the cacti; it's long on scenic splendour, but short on eligible men. You can go miles through the Chiricahua Forest or the Apache reservation without seeing one! I didn't trek down into the Grand Canyon either, because I thought there wouldn't be many chances of research there. And the big towns like Phoenix are Sunset Cities for geriatrics, because the climate is so wonderful (though it's getting very hot now). So I ended up in Sedona, Oak Creek Canyon, where it's cooler and seems to have a healthy male population. Also, there are lots of good restaurants and my hotel has a pool and a jacuzzi, so I thought I'd stay here and pamper myself.

After a day or two lying by the poolside I got tired of men staring at my tits. The crunch came when two of them took to torpedoing me from underneath while I floated on my front around the pool. They'd dive in like swallows and swoop up under me, so as to brush my boobs with their hands or back. If someone did that sort of thing on the underground, you'd call him a *frotteur*. (By the way, have you covered that in the Project?) I suppose it's one of the hazards of being well-stacked, but anyway, I decided to leave them to touch up the lesser talent and went off to do the sights. The Canyon is like Monument Valley on a smaller scale. Great piles of red stones rise out of the landscape with no rhyme or reason. There are lots that look like giant cocks, and you can see why the native Indians thought the place was sacred, with all these fertility symbols lying around. But, see one canyon and you've seen them all, so I went round the town to see what action there was. I saw a lot of bright purple jeeps parked together under a sign saying 'Purple People Promotions'. I went over to investigate and the most gorgeous man I've ever seen in my life – except for Scott – leaned down from the driving seat of one and said, 'Give you a ride, ma'am?' You remember Robert Redford in *Butch Cassidy and the Sundance Kid*? Well, multiply the Redford factor by ten and you get some idea. He was tall, with some good muscles, and had that sun-bleached streaky blond hair and wide blue eyes and a tender sort of mouth, half-smiling. I stopped in my tracks and said, 'Are you offering one?' 'Sure, jump in,' he said. 'I'll drive you any place you like. They just cancelled the party I was taking, but they still had to pay me, so I'm free. And you look like a nice lady, needing a ride.'

I got in and he drove through town and up the steep Canyon towards Flagstaff. He turned out to be a post-graduate student at some mid-West university who drove a jeep during vacations to make some dough. What he was studying was – wait for it! – Theology and Astrology, with Folklore as a subsidiary subject. I asked him about Voodoo, but he discounted it as pure superstition. After a while he said, 'Hey! Reckon I'll take you on the "Touch the Earth" tour.'

'What's that?'

'That's the Vortex Mystery tour. The Canyon is full of vortexes.'

'But what are vortexes?' He told me that they are magical energy spots on the earth's surface. In a valley or

149

on a mountain or in a lake, there are centres of force where energy lines meet. I wasn't convinced that I wanted to see these, but he was persuasive.

'You really get to renew your life forces when you hit one of these. Being around them just spaces me out. You'll see.' He really seemed to believe in all this nonsense. If you'd met him in 1968, you'd have called him a hippy – he had that "love, peace, man" serenity about him, and was wearing a string of Indian beads over his T-shirt, and a pair of faded, patched jeans. But he was butch, too, and his arms were wonderful – all tanned and muscular.

Suddenly he turned the Jeep off the road and drove straight up the steep hillside, following a track carved in the soft stone. It was bumpy and I was thrown up against him. 'Hang on,' he shouted and I did – I hung on to his chest, because I was lying on his shoulder. After a mile or two, we drove between two high, jutting rocks and stopped in a kind of glade with tall rocky walls which had a few shrubs dotted around the edges. I sat up straight again and we got out. In the middle was a round pool, forty feet across, maybe, and deep blue. We looked at each other's reflections as we bent over it. He was laughing. 'Feel anything?' I was feeling something – tension, you might say – but it didn't have anything to do with the vortex. 'Not yet,' I said.

'That's because we didn't hit the centre yet.'

'Where is the centre of the vortex?'

'In the middle of the pool. You got to swim.' He started to take off his clothes, but left on his underpants. His body was like a sculpture, and he dived into the pool like a flying fish. He came up near the middle and floated on his back.

'I can feel it right here, and it's spooky. Come on in and try.'

I had nothing under my shorts and sweatshirt, but it was a lonely spot. When I'd undressed, I jumped in and swam to join him. The water was warm and we floated side by side for some time. He had his eyes shut and he was smiling and humming to himself. The vortex started to work on me. I felt a strange impulse which seemed to be centred in my clitoris and some inexplicable line of force picked up my hand and put it down on his cock which I could see through his wet, transparent underpants. I felt a quite different force-line at work there, moving his cock under my hand. 'The forces are with us,' he said dreamily. The mysterious energy would not relinquish my hand, and, quite without meaning to, I started to massage his cock, which I could feel stirring magically. He rolled over in the water, propelled by powers beyond his control, and put his arms round me and clamped his lips to my breast. 'The Power is in you too,' he said.

It's hard to make love in deep water, so we swam back to the side and got out.

'There are more energy lines here,' he said, leading me through the bushes to a grassy hollow bathed in sun. He took off his underpants and his cock leapt out at me, a deeper brown than his body, but sculpted with equal care, although the artist had let his imagination run away with him where the proportions were concerned. But after looking at nothing but Saguaro cactuses for days, with their branching, multiplying, burgeoning phalluses, I could accept the exaggeration. We lay down in the grass and the sun beat down on us and insects buzzed round us. A smell of some odorous plant floated in the air.

There was no noise and no movement there, but the forces were still at work, making his cock rise and butt against my belly. I took it in my hand and then into my mouth, while he turned round to put his mouth between my legs. He nibbled my pussy-fur lazily and wrapped his mouth over my mound of Venus, then reached out a long tongue to tickle my clitoris. The energy field seemed static and held us like that for a long time. I sucked at him like a candy-stick and pushed back his foreskin with my tongue, rejoicing in the smooth round bulb with its tiny hole. It seemed to taste of the sun, the sea, the desert. It jerked around in my mouth while, down below, my clit responded as he suckled it and generated a magnetic field of its own. The magnetism grew until he turned turtle and I was suddenly on top of him, and his cock was drawn up into my cunt as if by a mysterious counter-gravity. I floated up and down on top of him and saw the grass and the yellow butterflies, while he looked up, wide-eyed, at the cloudless sky. Although we are made of clay, we two seemed to be dissolving into a watery element, and my cunt enveloped him as the sea wraps itself round a swimmer. We fucked for a long time as the energy washed through us and his hand supported my tits from below, and gently pinched my nipples until they became magnetic pleasure-vortexes too.

All the while, a rising tidal-wave of tension grew in us and at last it broke, and we were grappling with each other like mud-wrestlers, and turning over so that he could ride me. He plunged his tool into me as if he would never stop, and then at last we were both crying out our joy to the birds as his cock thrashed around inside me, sending out its riotous tide of sperm, and his coming touched the hidden vortex of my womb and sent pleasure whirling through my body until I was dizzy from the waves of it.

Well, Celeste, writing about that – which happened two days ago – has awakened the poet in me! I still think that the vital force is the one between men and women: vortexes just stir it up a bit. I did remember to ask this Gerry about his fantasies. As you can guess, what he dreams of is fucking in the open air – in the sea, in forests, anywhere where he can see the sky and feel the heat of the sun. But he's earthy too, and he admitted that he'd planned to screw me as soon as he saw me walking down the main street. Fantastic!

So now I must pack and get to the airport. More news from the Bay of Cortez. I plan to go to Puerto Kino and find out all about Mexican beach-combers. Please cable me $1000 URGENTLY, at the Holiday Inn, Hermosillo, Sonora Province, plus send two bras, 38 C cup – hard to get them big enough in this territory.

Yours,
Justine

11

A Day In The Life of Celeste

Christ what a day pissed with rain no bloody taxis and
the car on the blink. And Ivo – that little beast had better
watch his little arse in his new silky cords. Must have
been out of my mind tarting him up like that . . . fancies
himself too much already oily little tramp. Well it didn't
start off too badly. Got Justine's stuff in from New
Orleans in time to read it over. The guys over there seem
to be doing it like rabbits – time of her life she's having I
shouldn't wonder. But the expense! I've got to watch
that. She's spending twice as much as I do and I'm
bloody well not going to let her get away with that trip to
Mexico. Research my foot, mansearch more likely. If
only she'd get her work down in the proper format so we
could analyse it properly and cut out the literature.
You'd think she was practising to put books of her own
out, as if there wasn't enough porn out there already
what with me and the Roman orgy bloke and Xaviera
and Shirley and that nasty chap Cock something not to
mention all the mags. Well anyway I liked her bit about
the five-mile high wank only if it was me I think I would
have gone up and done the captain. Make his joystick
your toystick as you might say.

Well Ivo did nothing but sulk all round the shops and he was totally feeble about getting us taxis you'd think he was some kind of fairy always getting shoved out of the way by all and sundry. Wittering away about he wanted that grey silk. Well I told him before we went out that it was black or black and that was it. Not as if he ever buys himself a pair of socks. And when did he last get me anything, I ask. Well not since Christmas and what on earth he thought I'd do with all those ornament things those peculiar stone legs ... I mean with legs like I've got who needs legs? Anyway today it was just drip drip drip all morning and could he have cocoa at Fortnums just like a twelve-year-old. I did get him into the cords though and I thought God you little bugger you do fancy yourself don't you slinking around with your trim little arse and your cock showing through the material while you sit there slurping cocoa and me running late for V. I'll bite your fancy cock for you cords or no cords just see if I don't.

Just made it back in time for the big recruiting sergeant show. Sent Ivo off to get the car fixed no questions no buts I'm busy so there. So in she comes just a moment later carrying a big big silver plastic grip sort of thing. All bulgy and the zip undone in the rain. Oh my gosh here's 'The Wreck of the Hesperus' or one of the survivors anyhow I thought and *'Bonjour, Mademoiselle. Entrez, entrez, je vous en prie. Je suis désolée de notre temps Anglais si affreux'*. But back she comes with 'Good morning Miss Arden. It is for me a great privilege to make your acquaintance' and from then on we made it quite easily in English. It turns out JS had had the sauce to send her a copy of DFW he'd nicked off me and would you believe she had recognised herself straight off after all the trouble I'd taken. Since then apparently she's just gone on and on at JS trying to meet me. All this time she's been at Royal doing sociology with that pompous old dodo Morgan and having it off with JS no less in that poky little love nest of his on the canal. Same place he took me to straight from Heathrow the day we met in France on the train. God I've just remembered it was that weekend I snitched his diary and then I wrote up a chapter or two from it and he laughed so much when he read it and said 'Oh well you go ahead then. Probably write it better than I could'. So I did and hello Fame.

Well this Virginie – it turns out she's actually Véronique but I suppose JS wasn't on oath. So what if he didn't level in his diary – well anyway she's pretty much like I'd imagined. Fair hair, not very tall, looks an utter heap but you can see she's got a trim little fanny under this sort of woolly sack of a one-piece all pulled down by the wet. When I got it off her to put her in something of mine I could see her tits were pretty terrific and I thought let's have a look at that peach-coloured bum of yours my girl so I said you'd better borrow some dry pants too while you're at it and of course she turned round to put them on and oh my I thought they really are quite something aren't they meaning her bum cheeks and peach-coloured was just about right. Quite a raver too you can see the pink cunt lips when she bends down just like JS said you could. Anyhow her legs aren't as nice as mine 'cos they're on the short side. It looks as if she shaves them with the garden shears or something. Well I said let's have a drink and she said okay so we had Scotch while we chatted. And you know the thing is she's really quite bright I don't mean academic but she seems quick on the uptake. JS had shown her my ad from the

156

Staggers and told her here's your chance just answer this and see what happens but she sussed it was me without him telling her.

Apparently she thinks this is just her scene and it would be too I should think because she's the sort of girl who ... well, not to put too fine a point on it I should think with tits like those she would get in just about anywhere if I can once get her to dress properly. She really needs something quite filmy – green I think probably – so her nice long tits would show through and the men wouldn't notice those legs so much. The other thing is it turns out she really did do an awful lot at the French château. Most weekends in fact once she'd got herself settled in at her Lycée or École or whatever in Paris and there were her parents stuck down in Alsace thinking no harm and praying for some saint to protect her virginity. Well I thought you'd need two saints for that – one in the bows and one in the stern as an old sailor chap I knew said once. And she really did meet vast numbers of quite okay men there and got on fine with them in spite of her rather odd chambermaid act she always put on. You've got to remember a lot of men seem to panic about any actual women they might meet around the place at someone's house or a dance or wherever. Probably they get reminded of their mothers and sisters and what they need is someone a bit more like the apple-cheeked wenches who used to be their nannies. Scrub their cocks and ream out their little arseholes for them. So from then on it's chambermaids. It's a bit like that in France too apparently and that's how this Véronique got her act together. But the other thing about her which really makes me think she would do for me, apart from all that experience etc, is that she truly

157

seems to like the whole business and in fact she even made me laugh quite a bit. Well for instance she told me this one about the old French colonel.

What happened was that this old boy had spent the whole war bottled up in some prison camp and never really got his chance to do anything at all military. So although he did get promoted and everything in the end he still wanted everyone to think he was General de Gaulle taking on Rommel in the Western desert. So with her all he did was jump on her and ride her around the floor like a toy tractor, knees round her waist and his balls sort of squished under him on that bum of hers. Meanwhile he was jerking away at his cock like crazy, firing off salvoes of spunk at all the enemy tanks namely those old tapestry chairs they've got at the château. Véronique had to whirr and grind away under him making out she'd got caterpillar whatsits. Then she had to jump up as soon as the colonel had fired off all his ammo, and climb up on a stool wearing one of those black berets and a tricolour sash. And would you believe she had to pin these medals he always carried about with him straight into his chest while she kissed him on each cheek, and the old so-and-so stood there with tears in his eyes, saluting her with one hand while he tried to get his thing back up with the other. Talk about *splendeurs militaires!*

Well with all that going for her I thought no harm in offering her the job. I'm thinking of firing Lilac anyway and I damn well will if Ivo's been doing her behind my back. The long and the short of it is Véro's starting next weekend and I'm putting her straight in. No practice with Ivo though ... well I mean she doesn't really need it does she? I've given her all the forms and that reminds

158

me she'll need at least two hundred to get some clothes. I can't have my girls going around in Oxfam stuff.

JS got on the line just as she was going, and I wondered whether to break the news. But he went straight in with both feet and more or less begged me to take her. You know I really do wonder about men sometimes. What ever happened to good old-fashioned monogamy and jealousy and all that? Anyway I told him she was in and he seemed really happy. What are you going to fantasise about all night when you know she's out on an assignment I wondered and then I thought well that's a good idea I'll ask him one day since he thinks he owes me lunch. Anyway, he wanted to know who his first contact would be and I told him I was keeping him on ice till the right moment.

Couldn't make it with him to the Grenadier in the end 'cos it was getting late and anyway I'd had one or two already. So it was heigh-ho and off to Norm's for my pampering session. One of these days I'm going to write Norm up because really his place is quite amazing. I mean where on earth are you going to find a hairdresser with unisex jacuzzis, his and hers dildoes all with his customers' initials just in case, naked twelve-year-old Filipinas doing your toe-nails, and lovely old Norm himself? Always pretending to be a raving old poof but actually that shaft of his has been up more women than I've had men, and he has this way of standing next to you with his fingers on the back of your neck and his shaft comes under the chair arm and takes you just under your ribs and you think my god he must be 60 at least and he's still at it. No I don't think I will do it. They'd probably close him down and Stephen Ward him and then it would be all about half the Cabinet and three judges have got wives who go there not to mention all the East European embassy lot. So no Norm in this new book I'm doing.

Today it was pretty terrific. I was feeling all damp and steamy from dashing around so I thought let's start in the jacuzzi and one of the girls can do my toes while I'm in there. So Norm lets me have the one I like and I lie back on a shelf and stick my legs up on the edge so she can get at them. This puts my cunt right up against one of the jets, so I have to turn the tap down a bit because it was a bit strong to begin with. My goodness though. Once I'd got it right it was utterly fab. The jet was still strong enough to push the folds back round my clit, and it rippled up over me there with a lovely sort of throbby trickle. I could see my cunt hair all flowing out straight with the current, and the stream kept right on over me until it tickled my tits. I thought I'd better keep my cunt shut for starters, so I put a hand under my bum and pinched the flaps together.

There were only two other people there. One of them I didn't know, but he was dead to the world lying on his front on top of one of the vertical jets. Having the time of his life to judge from the way his buttocks were clenching and unclenching themselves. Probably one of those merchant wankers I thought. The other guy was pretty far gone too. He'd got the most terrific cockstand you've ever seen and in fact that's how I recognised him since lying down where I was I couldn't see his face. Anyway I thought here's a good tease so I rolled over a bit to look him straight in the cock and said 'I believe we've met before, haven't we?' Well he knew I couldn't have seen his face since he couldn't see mine, but it still took a while for the penny to drop. And then of course the joke was he couldn't make up his mind whether to keep his hand on his cock for the sake of camouflage, or whether to remove it because I'd caught him wanking. Anyway at Norm's the rule is no names, apart from Norm himself of course, so I couldn't introduce myself. Instead I just reached out my free hand and gave his balls a friendly squeeze. That reminded him of something all right. So I put on my demure voice and said 'Quiet in the British Library today, is it then?' Do you know I really swear it's the only time I've seen a cock blush. All of a sudden this great cock of his subsides like a punctured barrage balloon, just as Norm prances in with a tray of goodies. So we all sit up and play grown-up tea parties ever so correct, while I use a leg to push my Filipina up against Hengist's thigh. Hurrah I thought. This is definitely one for the diary. I'll leave a note for him in the library tomorrow to remind him to be more honest about his fantasies in future.

Things got a lot more frantic then as men kept on coming in from late lunches. Most of them were in no state to work anyhow, and the sight of all those drink-sodden cocks got a bit too much for me. So I let Norm take me off and do my hair. He's done it streaky again, the way I had it when I met JS. Afterwards he sat and chatted while I dried out, then he went and fixed me up with one of those airline headsets and played me that naughty song of Alberta Hunter's. 'Send me a Man', is it? Norm himself is really one of those men who knows how to use his head in an emergency.

Well that brings me more or less to where I am now really, 'cos all I did after Norm's was come straight home to read my post and get this diary up to date. That Ivo creature is really trying to bug me I think. First of all he'd taken the telephone off the answering machine so I didn't get the call I've been waiting for from the film company. Then he'd left all the ice out in a jug and it had all melted away during the afternoon and there was none left in the fridge. His idea of my supper was two cucumber sandwiches with crusts on. Cut thick just to make sure I got the message. Then he'd gone and got penitent at the last minute and stuck a fat pink rose into a nice big hunk of chocolate cake for me.

Then there is one thing I should mention really to be honest only I don't know why it just slipped my mind. Probably sort of repressed I suppose. Just fancy! Me of all people. What happened was that V. came past. Said she'd forgotten her silver thing and there it was staring you in the face in my hall. I thought she was really after something else but couldn't think what at first. She had her little legs up on my sofa while we had a drink together and I was looking at all that fuzz on her calves. So I said Véronique would you let me do something for you and I suddenly saw my hand had gone off on its own and there it was lying on one of her knees. I thought oh Christ no, not that but she just put her hand on mine and pressed it and lifted it further up her thigh and it was so soft and lovely and then I realised why she'd come back and we went into my room. And afterwards I gave her a bath and while she was lying in it I sat on the edge and got my hands all soapy and picked up her legs and lathered them. Then I reached over for my razor and mowed her legs with it right up to her cunt and all the time I let my toes play around in her cunt fur. She was lying back all dreamy, with her arms on the sides of the bath and a hand resting gently on my thigh. When I had finished I sponged her legs down with a flannel and then I let my hands slide up and down them, feeling the new baby skin all fresh and delicate and smooth. Really I wonder whether I don't perhaps think girls are my thing. Well I was thinking that when I suddenly heard myself saying quite gruffly, 'Time you were off now. For God's sake hurry up and get dressed, and I'll ring you tomorrow.' She looked as if I'd kicked her for a moment, but then she gave a little shrug and got into her clothes. I tried to beg a kiss before she left, and now I keep on seeing her lips pouting at me the way they did when she reversed out of the front door.

There was no note from Ivo to say when he's getting back of course, so since it's gone eleven I'm bloody well going to ring Lilac here and now and see if they're at it together.

Later now. Well, probably a bad idea but I rang up that slut Lilac pretending it was about instructions for her first interview and I do give her the info on that eighty-year-old though I don't tell her he's old and only gets it up once a month or so and that'll serve her right for slavering after slinky young arses and lissom cocks. She's sweet as sugar on the phone – a bit breathless like she always is, stupid bitch, but while we're talking I hear a man groan near the phone all passion and anguish, like he's just coming, and I'd recognise that groan anywhere so I ring off without saying any more and then the brandy bottle is still half full so I pour myself one and then another and another and oh shit where's the diary got to remember to get some tomorrow.

I know what I'd like to do to that Ivo if I was Cockburn and then I have another and very tired now so I think I'll go to bed and wank, see if there's any life left down there . . .

163

12

Psycho-Sexology

Celeste was always in a bad mood after reading a report
from Justine. So when Ivo came in the next evening,
having wisely stayed out all day, he found her in the
study bent over Justine's letter in a state of rage, snorting
'I'll give her "rosebud opening" and "tidal wave of
tension"! What an insufferable romantic she is! It shows
that once you fall in love you lose all scientific objectivity.
And why can't she ever fill in the proper forms?' He
didn't associate her anger with the phone call to Lilac the
night before, and he tried to cheer her up by proposing a
trip to her favourite restaurant in Kensington. She
agreed sullenly, and they ended up spending too much
money – so Celeste said, pointing out that it was all hers –
and drinking too much, and quarrelling over whether
Kinsey had got it right about prostitutes when he said
that 'upper-level men' went to tarts because they could
do things with them that their wives would not permit.
Ivo thought that any woman would let her man kiss her
breasts, but Celeste said she knew a lot of women who
hated it. Then they quarrelled about Ivo's allowance and
she made some unpleasant allusions to what he spent it
on. By the time they'd got to their second brandy, he

wished he was somewhere else. Celeste paid and they took the Underground home because she said, untruly, that she had forgotten to bring enough taxi money.

As they walked down the road towards the house, an extraordinary figure confronted them. He was a handsome young man, with African or Indian blood in him, and wild, curly black hair. He was wearing a jacket with shoulder-pads six inches wide, tightly fitted at the waist and striped in black and shiny gold, and a black leotard. Ivo admired his style. The man stopped them at the steps to the door and asked if they knew of any parties in the area.

'Wish I did,' said Ivo mournfully. 'Why?'

'Because I'm a stripper,' said the man, 'and I'm looking for somewhere to do my act.'

'Come in,' said Celeste. 'It's too late for parties but maybe you can entertain us privately.'

He seemed to like the idea, so they went in, up to the red drawing-room. The light there was very soft and there were great piles of multicoloured velvet cushions and two low sofas, and a table of bottles and glasses. Ivo poured more brandy and Celeste asked the man his name, and how he came to be a stripper.

'I'm Marco. I've been on this game for a year. The hours are good and it pays better than driving a van.'

'Would you tell us a bit about it? You needn't strip, but I'll pay you the same fee, whatever it is.'

'Fifty quid is the usual. Yes, for that I'll tell you anything!'

'Just tell us about your act, and why you do it.'

'Well, I go into some party – I prefer a gay scene, but I'll do it in front of straights too. I have my tapes with me and I dance to them and take off my gear, just like a woman stripper. Why do I do it? Really, it's to turn myself on. I like to have guys looking at my body and imagining what it would be like to make it with me. While I'm doing it I often get a big stiff hard-on, just at the thought, and the audience likes that even better.'

He did have a lithe, well-built body and both Celeste and Ivo were wondering separately what his erection would be like.

'So, are you gay?'

'I don't know. AC/DC maybe. I've been with lots of men, but I've had some women too. On the whole, I prefer guys. There are more things you can do with them.'

Celeste explained about Project Fantasy Uncover and asked Marco to tell them if he had any fantasies. Ivo was sprawled across a heap of cushions, and his eyes never left the stripper's face as he spoke.

'First of all, there's the sort of guy who turns me on – I can tell you about that. He's big, not tall maybe, but very stocky – he's probably done lots of weight-training, and has got himself amazing muscles, big as sweet potatoes. He looks as if he's just walked off of a building site. He's wearing a white sweatshirt, torn across the chest, so that I can see that he's very hairy, and a pair of ripped jeans, and sneakers. You can see his prick standing up beside his flies. He has fair hair, cut very short – sort of butch.'

'How does the fantasy go on? What happens?'

'I imagine that he's coming to my house to build a wall. He's working in the back-garden and has to bring all his tools and bricks through. The passage is very narrow and when he comes past he brushes against my bare arm. Then he comes past again and this time he brushes against my crotch with his leg. But I have no

166

idea whether he's into men, or completely straight. Later on, he comes into the kitchen, hot and sweaty, and I give him some tea – and when I hand it to him our fingers touch. And this goes on all day, maybe for several days. We keep touching each other by accident, but I think he might be doing it on purpose. Is he or isn't he? Would he or wouldn't he? The end of the fantasy is that I'm taking a shower in the downstairs bathroom, but I leave the door unlocked. He comes in without knocking and I don't hear him. He takes off his jeans and the first thing I know is that he's stepping into the shower behind me and pressing his big hard-on against me. Then I know that he wants it too.'

Soon after telling his tale, Marco left, pleased with his evening's earnings. Celeste went to her office to take some notes, then came up to Ivo's bedroom. He was lying, curled up into a small, tender ball, on his bed. Her mood had changed rapidly, and she looked at Ivo with a warm, loving, longing look in her eyes. But he didn't look at her.

'Celeste,' he said, 'I've got something to tell you. I think I might be gay.'

'Don't be so idiotic! You know how much you like fucking women.'

'Yes, but really, when I looked at Marco's body and heard him talk, I felt a funny kind of excitement, and I got a hard-on.' Celeste had noticed this and had thought that she had something to do with it. She hid her feelings in an outburst of anger.

'Of all the self-indulgent, imbecile, narcissistic, cunt-struck men I've known, you're the worst. Go and find out, then. Why don't you go off to the Fallen Angel and get yourself laid?'

She strode out and Ivo lay looking woeful for a long time before he went to bed and consoled himself with his favourite childhood book, *Wind in the Willows*. He liked the picture of the Great God Pan.

The next day he went out before breakfast without leaving a note. Celeste was half glad not to have to deal with him. She put on a very short yellow shift and combed her hair so that it stuck out like a lion's mane. Then she had coffee and croissants and went down to her office. She spent the morning making notes for a draft of the first chapter of the final Report. She also spent some time devising a form to give her researchers. If she could make them all fill it in, it would concentrate the minds of scatterbrains like Justine on the task in hand. [The form is reproduced on the opposite page.]:

Celeste was surveying the form with satisfaction when the doorbell rang and there was Herr Doktor Müller, who had taken up her invitation to visit the Foundation. She took him downstairs to look at the Museum. His name was Karl, and he was a clean-shaven, blond man in his late thirties, but boyish – very much your ideal Aryan man. But he dressed appallingly, Celeste decided, looking at his loud check suit, and his massive black glasses, and he was all hunched up as if frightened of something. He started looking earnestly at the collection of sex artefacts. The long, hollow wooden tubes puzzled him. Celeste explained how, in some tribes, young boys had been made to wear them on their penises, strapped round their buttocks, from the age of eight onwards. The theory was that, because the tube was thin, the penis would grown in length rather than width. Periodically, when the knob of the penis showed at the top, the tube was changed for a longer one and the process began

THE ARDEN FOUNDATION FOR SEXUAL RESEARCH
Project Fantasy Uncover – Time Sheet

RESEARCHER   DATE   REFERENCE

PLACE   TIME ON   TIME OFF   TOTAL HOURS
                                       ON TASK

SUBJECT   SEX   AGE   HEALTH   NATIONALITY

COCK DIMENSIONS (if applicable)   Normal   Aroused

                          Length
                          Circumference

(Note: give best estimate if no accurate measurements available)

FANTASY   HARDWARE   ORGASMS/   TOTAL
                         HOUR   ORGASMS

                                     (1) Subject
                                     (2) Researcher

TARTS   Yes/No – delete as applicable

BRIEF COMMENT

EXPENSES CLAIMED

                                                        TOTALS

Hotels
Travel
Entertainment
Clothes
Postage
Stationery
Telephone
Other (including appliances)

                        TOTAL EXPENSES CLAIMED

FOR OFFICE USE ONLY. DO NOT WRITE ON THIS SECTION

FANTASY   HARDWARE   ENTERED
CODING   CODING   DATABASE

EXPENSES:

                     Allowed this period:
                     Carried forward:
                     LESS advances:
                     _____

                     Total credits:

Expenses/orgasm   Expenses/hour

---

again, until the boy was about sixteen. It had worked, apparently, and produced men with very thin cocks, ten or twelve inches long, which could penetrate so far as to give women cervical orgasms. 'Or so said the European travellers who visited these tribes and discovered the custom, but I don't believe it,' said Celeste. '*Sehr interessant*,' said Doctor Müller, and made a note in his diary.

Then there were the metal cylinders with callipers attached which measured the dimensions of a man's penis, when flaccid and when aroused. The modern version, which the Museum also boasted, and which Celeste had originally bought for her researchers, worked through a flexible rubber tube and a dial.

'Really? I would think that the process would be too exciting for a true measurement of the flaccid penis,' said Doktor Müller. Celeste noted his reply, with half an eye on his trouser-bulge. They moved on to look at a shelf of ornaments, as they first seemed to be. Actually, these were not ornaments but about twenty cock-shaped implements, bought by Celeste in a Sotheby's sale. They had been made before the First World War by a famous prostitute in Vienna, whose clientele included members of most of the European royal families.

'She aroused them,' said Celeste, 'and then put butter on their cocks and then wrapped a soft plaster mixture round the penis. It dried very fast, and slipped off quite easily. Then the moulds were used to make casts.'

The cocks were made in a light alloy, and the range of shape and sizes was baffling.

'She used the casts to blackmail her customers later on, and one of them was the prize exhibit in a famous divorce case. It's all in her memoirs – you should read

171

them.' Celeste added, 'Actually, I'm thinking of going into business to reproduce them in plastic as dildoes. Imagine the satisfaction of being able to wank yourself with a Rumanian prince's cock!' Doktor Müller had little sense of humour. He did not respond, but went on to study some of the more inexplicable items in the collection. There were cylinders for fitting over a man's penis during intercourse, to prevent full entry into the vagina.

'A common way of preserving the girl's virginity in some cultures was to use one of these,' said Celeste. 'The man felt as if he were inside the woman, because of the friction against the cylinder, which had had oil poured into it. But he couldn't penetrate the hymen, even if he lost control.'

The various implements for anal penetration were also of great interest to Herr Doktor Müller. 'Do you mean that any man would want this inside him?' he asked, gesturing at a large, black rubber dildo with straps to hold it in position round the hips. 'Incredible!'

'Not really,' said Celeste, thinking of Godolphin Grackle, whose brass throne she was hoping to have copied for her Museum by an obliging ironmonger. 'Some men like that – and they're not always gay, by any means. If you put one of these on, you just need to sit in a rocking chair or ride a bicycle to get the most fantastic turn-on – or so I'm told.' Doktor Müller looked at her speculatively.

She went to make him a cup of coffee and when she came back he was sitting on Ivo's couch. She screwed up her courage and said, 'Now that you're here, can I recruit you for the Project and ask you a few questions? It's all strictly anonymous, you understand, and I would like to find out what makes a psycho-sexologist tick.' He seemed flattered, and agreed. They got through the preliminary questions swiftly – he was married, never used prostitutes, sometimes imagined his penis as a lighthouse, and so on. Doktor Müller was a well-behaved subject and replied as if he were dictating the answers to his income tax form. But when it came to the question about fantasies, he looked over at her and said, 'I have a fantasy to show you. Is it permitted?'

'Of course,' said Celeste, steeling herself for the worst. But Doktor Müller lay quietly down at full length on the couch, his head resting on the arm. 'Please sit on a chair behind my head,' he said, 'like the Freudian analyst. Now ask me some questions and I will show you what I fantasise about.' While she was going through a particularly mundane section of the questionnaire, she saw him open his flies and put his hand in to take out his thingummy. He was quite well-hung, and the bulge she had noticed did not lie – he already had a hard-on. He was stroking his prick with one hand and holding it vertical with the other, so that he could see what was happening. Celeste considerately reached over to spotlight it for him with her adjustable desk-top lamp.

'I like to do this with a beautiful woman watching me,' said Doktor Müller. 'I also like to think that she is doing the same herself, while she lusts after me. Are you doing that? Let me hear you, please.'

Celeste was never averse to an invitation to put her hand between her legs. Luckily she had no briefs on under her shift, and could slip her fingers up to her pussy with ease. Down there, she felt a warm, friendly dampness – she sighed a little as she touched herself. Doktor Müller moaned in sympathy and redoubled his efforts, his hand rocketing up and down now. 'What do you do now?' he asked, his eyes shut.

'Me? Oh, I'm slipping two fingers in, one on each side of my clitoris. It's very wet there now and there's no friction, but they slide along it like a ski over the snow. I am feeling a delicious twitching in my shaft.'

'Ach so! Shaft! All women like to think of their clitoris *wie ein Schwanz* – I mean like a penis. Freud was so right,' observed Doktor Müller, rocking his from side to side and writhing desperately on the couch. Celeste emitted a few loud groans to encourage him and found that her finger was sliding into the deep cleft between her labia, although she had not told it to.

'He was wrong,' she gasped. 'We think of it as our clit. We don't need penises, it's quite good enough – OH!' She recovered herself a little. 'Anyway, I'm asking the questions. How do you feel about what is happening to you now?'

Doktor Müller was pummelling his prick rapidly.

'Good,' he said.

'Do you feel guilty about it at all?'

'Not so guilty!' he said, waving it from side to side and wrapping his spare hand round his balls.

'Is this something you've done since you were a child?'

'Of course it is, pig-arse' he said breathlessly, giving his cock great, clenching squeezes.

'Good. I am glad that you called me pig-arse. You must learn to express your feelings.' Celeste couldn't say any more, because she was doubled up with silent laughter. Quite suddenly, the laugh in her belly tuned in to the wavelength of the throbbings in her cunt, and she felt it contract in blissful bouts of pleasure.

Doktor Müller was frantically frigging his prick now,

174

and he became even more frantic as he heard Celeste's involuntary moan. *'Ach, Himmel!'* he shrieked loudly. She watched as he gave his tortured prick one last twist, and a great jet of fluid shot up into the air – several inches, she estimated – and fell to rest on his trousers. He gave a grunt of satisfaction and was silent for a minute. Then he returned his cock to its hiding place and sat up, turning to look coolly at Celeste.

'That was an interesting experiment,' he said. 'Because never have I actually lived through this fantasy. I make love to my wife often, yes, and she always enjoys it. Sometimes she masturbates me, if she is tired. And when I am away from her I do it myself, though not often. But this experience is remarkable. I often wanted to do it, but I never found the woman who I could ask.'

Celeste wanted to know why he should have such a fantasy, but she decided against asking. Her own interpretation would probably be much more acute than his: an up-tight sex psychologist, who spends all his time resolving other people's problems, really needs to be analysed himself, makes great endeavours to have a proper, meaningful, progressive, sexually-fulfilling, problem-free relationship with his wife. No wonder that all he really wants to do is get his rocks off peacefully, with no one else's pleasure to consider, and no demands on him. He likes an onlooker, to serve as a confessor and absolver of his solitary sins, but he doesn't want to see her lest she might require some response from him. Very good, thought Celeste, pleased with herself. I wonder what credentials one needs to become a psycho-sexologist?

Before she showed him out, Doktor Müller said that he was the consultant for a forthcoming television programme about sexual behaviour. He thought she might be a suitable panellist. 'I have now read your book,' he announced, 'and I see that you have much to contribute to our psycho-sexual understanding.' Celeste thanked him for the suggestion, and he left, more jaunty and less hunched than before. She went back to her desk, picked up the phone and dialled a number. It was Cockburn's.

13

Lilac's First Assignment

Lilac had spoken to Mr Mortimer on the phone. She knew that he liked girls with brightly-coloured stockings and short skirts, so she arrived at his door wearing a scarlet mini-dress, which displayed her rump at its best, and matching stockings. She was very, very nervous, but Ivo had told her it would go fine. He didn't seem to know anything about Mr Mortimer, however; he must be off Celeste's secret list of respondents.

The house was in Chelsea, in a smart street, and as she knocked at the door, Lilac noticed that the knocker was brilliantly polished. A young woman in a black dress, not very pretty, answered the door, asked her name and said: 'I'll show you up. He's expecting you.' They went up the elegant staircase and Lilac was ushered into the front-room of the house, Mr Mortimer's study. It was full of antiques and old books and leather armchairs, and she was fascinated by the gilded statues of naked girls holding flambeaux, which served as lights. A voice spoke from deep in the armchair by the window. 'Excuse my not getting up. A bit unsteady on my legs these days.' She looked in that direction and saw an old man sitting there, almost lost in the huge chair. He was thin now, although he had clearly been a large man once. His hair was white and sparse, brushed back off his high forehead. He had a brown face with a million lines on it, and rivetting blue eyes. He fixed these on her as he said, 'Please sit down, Lilac. I may call you Lilac, may I? Celeste has told me all about you.' He was very courteous, but had a strong, authoritative voice.

'You might think I'm rather old for this sort of thing – I'm eighty. But I've known Celeste for many years. Her parents brought her to my Embassy when she was a mere child in pigtails and they were travelling in the East. We've kept in touch since then, and when she told me about the Project, I volunteered right away.'

Lilac was nonplussed. How could she begin to use the techniques that Samantha had shown her on Mr Mortimer? He seemed to be in command of the situation, however.

'Celeste said you might like to hear a few of my reminiscences, and I'm happy to oblige. There aren't many people around or still alive whom I can talk to about my rakish past. My wife's been dead ten years, but of course I couldn't tell her anyway.'

'Thank you. I'd like to hear your memories. I'll take some notes, if you don't mind.'

'Not at all. You might, for example, like to hear about my initiation. Yes? Then that's what I'll tell you. I was a young boy, eighteen or so. My father was wealthy and had got into the way of gambling. He took me round the casinos in all the best resorts of Europe that summer. That was the year I drove a bus in the General Strike, so I must have been eighteen. It was in Biarritz that I met an elderly man, some kind of German prince I think he was, but he was in exile now, naturally. He spoke first-rate English, and seemed to take a liking to me immediately. He invited me to go to his hotel suite one evening when my father was busy. The Prince had a whole floor of the hotel and there was a drawing-room, a dining-room, a study and various bedrooms, all very sumptuous and rococo. He gave me a glass of wine. I wasn't used to drinking in those days, so it went straight to my head. He showed me various treasures of his, and then he said: "Have you had anything to do with women – with girls?" The only girl I actually knew was my sister, and I said so. "Good," he said, "I have a treat in store for you. A lady of pleasure is due to arrive very soon. I want you to watch what happens." I had had another glass of wine by then, and I was confused about his meaning, but I thanked him for his kindness. There was a knock at the door then, and he quickly led me into an ante-room which was on the far side of the state bedroom, and told me to wait there and to remain quiet, whatever happened. I was to come and join him when he beckoned me.

'I sat on a hard chair in the ante-room, out of sight behind the door. There was a large gap between the door and the jamb, however, and I could see the room and the four-poster bed quite easily. I heard a woman's voice, and some conversation in German, and then footsteps coming into the bedroom. The next thing was, there was a ravishingly beautiful woman taking off all her clothes! She had masses of long, raven-black hair, looped in a fancy pattern of curls and ringlets on top of her head. She had a fine, pale face with very red cheeks and mouth, and she was wearing – or taking off, rather – a long scarlet dress, covered with frills and flounces. Underneath, she had on garters and red stockings like yours, my dear, and the sort of corset that women used to wear, black and stiff and laced up very tight. It forced her breasts up till they bulged and overflowed the top. The Prince had taken his trousers off too, and was wearing just a long shirt. He went and put his arms round her, and started kissing her neck where the hair was looped up from it, and then moved down to slaver over the tops of her breasts, those great milk-white spheres which were mesmerising me. I was agog! He put one hand on her corset and another between her legs – on her thigh, I supposed, and he seemed to be rubbing and stroking her. I saw one of her hands disappear under his shirt, and he exclaimed angrily in German, so she stopped.

'Then they went over to the bed together and she lay down, still wearing her corset and stockings, while he got on top of her. My eyes were on stalks as he moved up and down. I'd never been told properly about the birds and bees, you see. He reached out a hand now, and I saw him make a sign to me, so I tiptoed in and stood at the foot of the bed, hidden behind the drapes. I could see perfectly and I was looking down between the woman's legs at what they sometimes used to call a quim, though I didn't know the word then. Her cunt – as you say now – was bright pink, surrounded by a thicket of black hair. It looked like a pair of lips, smiling at me, and I felt a strange stirring in my groin, a feeling I'd had often in tight trousers, or in bed, but had never taken much notice of. We were late developers in those days, you see, although maybe we had more fun finding things out. I put my hand down on the sensitive place and felt through my trousers that I had a cock-stand. I'd had that before, too, but never with a woman in sight.

'From my grandstand view, I could see that the Prince

was not actually in physical contact with the woman's cunt – he was just going through the motions of fucking her. Presently, he got up off the bed and came round the end to me. We were both out of sight from where she lay. He put one finger on his lips for silence, and with the other hand he reached down and unbuttoned my trousers, indicating that I should take them off. I did. Then he pulled off my pants and put a large hot hand on my cock, and frigged it a little. It was lucky that I didn't come at once, being so unused to all this, but somehow I've always had great staying power in that area. The Prince whispered very quietly in my ear, "When I get on top of her again, come behind me and do the same."

'Then he climbed back on to the bed and resumed his heavings on top of the woman. This time, he over-acted and was jumping up and down wildly so that when I climbed on behind him she didn't feel the difference. Her eyes were shut, anyway. I imitated the Prince, and spread my legs apart so that they lay outside hers, and leaned forward, resting partly on his back. He took one of my hands and pulled it forward, and laid it against the smiling pink lips of her cunt. My goodness, I'd no idea that women's parts were so hot and steamy! I was fascinated and I felt around her cunt with delicate feather-touches, then probed a little more. I discovered that the lips came apart and that underneath them was a soft groove trickling with warm moisture. My fingers were playing around like this when the lady moaned a bit. I thought I must have hurt her, so I stopped.

'She said something in German, the Prince replied and then said in English, "Continue doing that, she likes it." She probably thought he spoke some loving endearment since she didn't understand English – so she still did not know that there was someone else in the bed. I put back my hand and felt around her private parts again. I discovered the hole which led inside her, and even pushed in my finger an inch or two. Then I got interested in her clitoris, which I could feel poking out, very thick and stiff, among the black curls. I ran my fingers up and down a bit, feeling how velvety and lively it was. Suddenly, she gave a series of sharp yelps, and called out *"Herr Gott!"*

'All this time, my cock was getting stiffer and almost sore with the need to come. But the Prince reached out a hand behind him and grabbed it, and pulled me forward by the cock, forcing it downwards. He had moved forward along the woman's body so that he crouched high over her chest, and there was room for me behind him. Luckily, the woman still had her eyes shut, and a contented expression on her face. The Prince dragged me forward until my cock was actually touching the woman's rosy wet labia. "Put it inside", the Prince said, in a cooing voice which the woman mistook for a compliment. I doubted if I could, or if it was right or healthy, but when my cock touched her soft place, it seemed to leap forward of its own accord, and it sank deep into her cunt, which gripped it like a soft, slippery hand. I didn't know what to do next – the most unbelievable, unfamiliar sensations were shooting through my loins and up my spinal cord. I felt sick with fear and utterly ecstatic, both at once. Some instinct told me to move inside her, so I pulled my cock out then pushed it back in, then went on doing that, imitating the sort of movements the Prince had been making a few minutes before. The woman was calling out strangely, but I couldn't think about that because suddenly there was an explosion inside me. It was like a red, searing flash that started at my cock and rose to my brain. I thought I must be dying. I fell forward and stopped thrusting, and I felt great gouts of spunk jetting out of me, up inside her.

'When she felt me falling on top of her, the woman opened her eyes and realised what had happened. The Prince got off her and sat on the edge of the bed. I did so too, blushing and covering my limp, wet cock with both my hands. She gave the Prince a severe talking to, nodding and gesturing at me. He translated. "She says I should not have tricked her so. She only comes to see me because I cannot really fuck now, and it is easy money. She does not expect to be fucked when she comes here. However, she thinks you are a very promising and a very pretty young man, so she forgives you. She wants to give you a kiss." I lay myself down beside the woman and she kissed me passionately with her full red lips, then put my hand on her breasts, which felt soft and liquid as they flowed out from the corset. I felt my cock getting stiff again already, and she put her hand on it and laughed. She pointed downwards – I was to fuck her again, she meant. This time my cock slid in with no fear, very easily because my spunk had lubricated her passage. I dug and delved in it and toiled away and managed to keep going for ten minutes or so, although I was dying to spend again. I could see that the Prince had raised his shirt and was wanking himself as I fucked his lady of pleasure; he reached out his other hand and took hold of my balls, squeezing and twisting them as I screwed her, and moving beside me in time with my thrusts. His movements accelerated, and suddenly he fell forward and I saw drops of spunk fall from his cock. This urged me on to greater efforts, and when I came it was with another earthquake inside my head and another cloud-burst inside her. Then I lay on the bed, quite unstrung.

'Later, I learned from a young friend of the Prince that he was virtually impotent, due to some horrible disease which plagued the lechers of the day and also, maybe, due to his love for old French brandy. The only way he could get an erection was if another man, or preferably a boy, would do the fucking for him. In my case, the excitement of initiating a novice had given him an orgasm. Usually he couldn't make it at all. A pity, because women were the love of his life.'

Lilac had been making notes. 'That's fascinating,' she said primly, although she was astounded by these revelations. Mr Mortimer leant towards her. 'You wouldn't like to feel me up a bit, would you? I'm no good these days, not like I used to be. But I still like a girl's hand on my little mouse.' Lilac drew up her chair to be beside him, and put her hand on his crotch. She felt something there, but it was not stiff. He moved her hand gently aside and opened his flies, then inserted her fingers and wrapped them round his cock. It felt warm but drowsy. She kept holding on to it, and he began to talk again.

'I won't bore you with all the details of my sex life. I had lots of women until I was married. Since I was in the Diplomatic Corps, I could have women of all shapes and hues, and I loved them all. But fucking was what I liked doing best – I never had much time for fantasising. Then when I was married I behaved myself, and hardly ever saw the street-walkers and other girls that I'd known before. But the war made a difference. I was in London while my wife and children had gone to the country. As you walked round London during the black-out, you

184

were always being accosted by prostitutes, and sometimes I went with them. But the most remarkable thing that ever happened to me was just after the war. I was still in Intelligence – I wasn't demobbed until later – and my family was still away. One night I went to a dance hall. It had just reopened, to great rejoicing, and there was a lot of revelry. People were still flushed with victory and were behaving more freely than before – hugging and kissing each other on any excuse.

'I went up to two girls who were sitting together, as they did in such places, and asked one of them to dance. She was tall and svelte, blond hair over one eye like the film stars had then. Her friend had short dark hair and looked annoyed when I asked her to dance, but she got up and we danced. She had a black satin full-length dress and she snuggled up against me as we danced, so that I could feel all of her through it, even her nipples. She was delicious and fragrant and she seemed to like me, so I was wondering how I could cajole her to come back to my flat. After several dances, I suggested it and she said that she'd like to, but must tell her friend. The friend – she was Diana and my girl was called Genevieve – looked sullen at first, then brightened up and said that was a good idea, and that she'd come too.

'This was not my idea of a good time, but we all went back to the flat together and I gave them a drink. They whispered to each other a bit, and then Diana said "we've got a plan. Would you like to go to bed with Genevieve?" I was taken aback by such forthrightness, but delighted. "Yes, very much," I replied. "You have to take me too," said Diana. I didn't know what to make of it, but we all went into the bedroom, and I started to undress while they watched and giggled. I was a fine

185

figure of a man in those days, and I didn't at all mind showing myself off to two girls, even if one of them seemed rather grim. I had a cock-stand at the very thought of the tall, blond girl and they both admired it and commented.

'Then I went to undress Genevieve and she stepped easily out of her clinging dress and underwear. She had a marvellous figure too, all tit and bum and a tiny waist between them. She came and lay down on the bed with me and I forgot Diana altogether while I made love to her. I touched her up a bit and kissed her breasts and face, and then I put my cock-stand inside her and we started fucking. She seemed to be enjoying me and I was going faster and faster when suddenly I felt a great weight land on my back. It was Diana. She'd hitched up her long dress and was straddled across me, as if I'd been a horse. She thrust when I thrust, and moved back when I withdrew. She was literally riding me into her friend: her lover really, but I hadn't realised before that they were a Sapphic couple, as we used to say.'

Lilac felt a stirring in Mr Mortimer's cock as he relived the incident – but nothing more. He sat upright in his chair and reached over to Lilac and put a gentle, wrinkled hand on her breasts and felt them for a moment.

'Those are nice,' he said, 'just like I remember breasts being when I was young.'

'I went on screwing Genevieve for hours, it seemed. Her cunt was warm and welcomed me more warmly every time I thrust myself inside her. In fact, I fucked her until she came, and I felt Diana go rigid on top of me. Then I rooted away like a truffle pig until I spent myself, and I fell over and Diana fell on top of me. She was very

186

cold and angry afterwards, although she said very little – angry with me for pleasuring her friend, angry with Genevieve for liking it. We had a few more drinks together and then they left. I never saw them again. But it's always been a fantasy – or perhaps a dream – of mine, to be ridden by a woman while I'm stallion to her mare, if you follow me.'

'Oh, yes,' said Lilac. She was wondering what to do next. Her hand inside his trousers could sense that he was still not erect – his cock was hardly stirring. She tried rubbing it a little, but he stopped her with a gesture.

'No need for that, Lilac,' he said softly. 'I can do it myself when I want to. I'm rather tired now, anyway, and so it's no good.'

Lilac withdrew her hand. It seemed the interview was at an end. She felt thwarted – she had so longed to try the things that Samantha had shown her. But he was adamant, though polite, that she should go.

'Give Celeste my love,' he said. 'And tell her that I still remember her in pigtails. What a little minx! You're a nice girl too. I hope you've got a good man and are happy like I was. Then you'll have some good memories, as I do.'

He seemed inclined to fall asleep, and only just roused himself to shake her hand. Lilac let herself out and went home. She had been moved by Mr Mortimer's stories and felt that a sexy life might lead someone to placid contentment in his eighties. But she was puzzled; she couldn't understand why Celeste had fixed for her to see Mr Mortimer of all people, when Ivo had said that she would be the star researcher. She felt that her charms could have been put to better use elsewhere.

In the taxi she was astonished to find that her thighs

were all cool and slippery where they touched above her stockings. Surely the old man's stories hadn't made her come?

14

Bearding the Giant

It was a dark and stormy afternoon when Celeste set out to drive to Bluebeard's Castle. That, anyhow, was how she had come to think of Cockburn's house, which actually bore the name of 'Camelot'. She drove an old, yellow E-type which quickly ate up the miles, and soon she was in open country. She was puzzling about Cockburn's psychic make-up. She only knew of him through his books, which she believed to be pointlessly cruel and sadistic. On the publishing grapevine she had learned that he was a hack journalist who made money by writing commissioned biographies of the famous, but that he'd made so much money from his pornographic books that he'd been able to buy a grand house in England and a villa in the South of France. During the phone call she had pretended to know nothing of his pornographic activities, and had said that she had chosen his name as one of her sample because he was a well-known journalist and in the right age-group. In reply, he had been polite and willing, but haughty, and had insisted on a fee for the interview. 'It's not my policy to give interviews for nothing. Otherwise I'd be pestered all the time.' He clearly saw himself as a literary giant, or genius, and this probably aroused her ire most of all. Actually she could not guess his age from his voice – it had been light but steely. She had halved the proposed fee, pointing out that her time was valuable too.

Celeste had dressed with care for the meeting, putting on thick black tights in lieu of trousers. She had knee-high boots with a furry cuff at the top. Tall sharp heels. Her jacket was also black and boyish, with exaggerated shoulders and a tight waist; it stopped half-way down her thighs. At the neck she had added a small tawny fox-fur, complete with head and four dangling pads. Celeste's mood as she drove further into Buckinghamshire was black, almost sadistic. Ivo had been out all night again and had scarcely uttered a word that morning except to contradict her when she blamed him for forgetting to order extra milk. He was still droning on about whether he was gay or not – he had been on the phone for hours that morning to one of his vapid friends, talking about what it was like to come out. However, the grim frame of mind in which all this had left her was the appropriate one for seeing Cockburn.

As she passed through the village near which Cockburn lived, the clouds burst and a torrent of rain came down. She turned left at the end of the village and drove along a winding uphill road. His house was at the top of the hill, he had said. There was a flash of lightning, illuminating the puce-coloured sky, and she saw a building perched on the top of the hill, with pinnacles and a turret. That must be 'Camelot'. She went right, at a sign which some local wag had altered to read 'Cumalot'. In a few minutes, she was turning into a gravelled drive and passing under an avenue of tall, dark fir-trees. The drive opened up into a wide paved courtyard – she had arrived. The house was a large Victorian Gothic construction of red brick, fancifully built, with battlements at the top and a tower at one end. The lightning played around its turret. Celeste grabbed her briefcase and made a dash through the rain for the front door – a vast, forbidding wooden thing, covered with black wrought-iron bolts and claw-shaped hinges, and twice her height. She reached up to pull the bell and heard a jangling sound inside. A moment later, the door swung open, creaking.

A man stood in the doorway and gestured her inside. 'I heard your car coming up the hill,' he said, 'so I came down from my tower to answer the door. I've given the servants the afternoon off.' Cockburn was a middle-aged man of middle height and slim build. His brown hair had receded a long way, leaving a shiny dome. He had a thin, chiselled face with a stern mouth, and the impression of ascetic severity was enhanced by his round, brown-rimmed spectacles. All told, a complete nonentity, was Celeste's verdict; you could pass him in the street without looking twice. On second thoughts, he did bear a strong resemblance to Christie, formerly of 10, Rillington Place but now resident at Madame Tussaud's. However, he had no whitewash brush in his hand. She stepped inside and shook the rain off like a cat. The door led directly into a large room with a great fireplace, a long dining table and a lot of uncomfortable looking chairs, patterned on mediaeval seats with hard, carved backs. There were some tapestries on the walls, which were faced with roughly hewn stone, and lit by wall lights shaped like flaring torches. The only thing which cheered the dismal place at all was the roaring log fire. Celeste went at once and stood beside it to dry herself.

'Thank you for seeing me at such short notice,' she began diplomatically. 'I didn't realise the weather would be so foul, though. What a drive!'

'I enjoy this kind of weather,' replied Cockburn, 'it suits my mood.' There was no obvious response to that, and Celeste had already decided not to waste time in polite conversation.

'The interview won't take more than an hour, I hope,' she said. 'I don't want to take up your valuable time.'

'That's quite all right. I set aside the whole afternoon for you.' He sounded gloating. 'Would you like to come up to my study? We can be cosy there.'

Cosy was not what she felt in Cockburn's company, but Celeste followed him down a corridor to a stone spiral staircase and upstairs to the first floor. A door led directly off the starcase, which continued on upwards, and they went through it into Cockburn's study. The room was pentagonal, so they must be in the tower. The study was what you might expect of any writer with a taste for the antique. There were great dark wooden bookcases, lined with leatherbound works, and two black armchairs by the coal fire. There was a large ebony desk, littered with papers, which looked out at a gloomy prospect of firs and cypresses. To its right was a small shelf filled with Cockburn's pornographic works, to judge by the garish covers, which contrasted with the more dignified volumes elsewhere in the room.

'You don't have a word processor?' asked Celeste, puzzled by the absence of what she considered to be the writer's most essential tool.

'I prefer to dictate my books to my secretary. She comes and sits by the fire, naked, with her long fair hair draped round her shoulders, and takes it all down in shorthand. I find that the sight of her inspires me to greater heights of creativity.' He gave her a tight-lipped, ironic smile.

They sat in the two armchairs and Celeste got out her clipboard and questionnaire. The first few questions went well enough: Cockburn was not married, nor attached to anyone, he freely admitted. He confessed to having used the services of prostitutes at times in the past, but not regularly. He said he certainly never read pornography, with such distaste that she believed him absolutely; he was clearly too complacent to care what other authors of his kind might write. And he had not lied, for after all writing is not reading. Yes, he had many fantasies and yes, he sometimes imagined his penis as some kind of sharp instrument, a corkscrew for example. The next question, which asked for a detailed account of the subject's fantasy, was in truth the only one to which Celeste ever wanted the answer. The others were mere padding. When she put the question, Cockburn immediately said 'I can show you what I mean much better if you come with me to the room upstairs.' This was said lightly, but Celeste found it ominous. She picked up her clipboard and followed him up the staircase into the room directly above the study.

The first thing she noticed was that this must be almost the top of the tower. A wooden ladder at one side of the room led up to a trap-door, and the ceiling was criss-crossed with the original heavy brown beams. The second thing was that there were numerous hooks embedded in the beams, with pulleys attached to them from which ropes were hanging down. The third thing she noticed was a series of black-framed engravings running all round the walls.

'Please feel free to look at my pictures,' said Cockburn, seeing the direction of her gaze. The first picture was of a naked girl, hung upside down by one foot from the ceiling. A naked man was raping her with a dildo while another naked girl wanked him over the hanging girl's breasts. Then, there were two girls and a man tied to diagonal wooden crosses, stood up against the wall of a building, with a man dressed in the garb of an eighteenth-century nobleman stabbing their bodies with a small knife.

'That was de Sade's favourite occupation,' said Cockburn as she examined it. Then she looked at a sketch of a wide gallows with three pulleys and three naked women hanging there, tits upwards, suspended by ropes around their waists. Two aristocrats, fully dressed but with vast, erect phalluses poking out from their breeches, were about to violate the women. Next was a repetitive series of drawings of men and women, all naked, splayed out on sofas, bottoms up, being beaten by noblemen wielding whips and switches, and there were several pictures of men and women heaped up together in acrobatic positions, with everyone licking or sucking someone else's genitals, while simultaneously being fucked or buggered. Celeste quickly passed by the picture of two women strapped to a sort of hydraulic press who were being lowered on to each other, apparently with a view to flattening them both, by gleeful satyrs; but she lingered at the final engraving in the series. This showed a girl – naked, of course – hung by both legs from the ceiling, with a man kissing her mouth while he fucked another girl, strapped on to a wheel beneath him, and pushed his hands into the cunts of two other women. He himself was being buggered by

194

the familiar, half-naked aristocrat. The details had been lovingly elaborated by the artist: the pulley-rope ran down and was hitched to the giant phallus of an atlantid who propped up the wall, balancing a basket of flowers on his head. Celeste had an unfamiliar feeling in her stomach, which she decided must be nausea.

'These are from the 1797 edition of *Juliette*, aren't they?' she asked.

'A woman after my own heart! Are you an admirer of de Sade as well?'

'I've read a few of his books,' answered Celeste, cautiously evading the nuance.

'Now let me show you some of my treasures. Then you'll begin to understand my fantasies better.'

The room was sparsely furnished. There were four wooden, brass-bround chests with great locks and a number of guns, swords and riding crops stapled around the walls. There was also a long, flat, bed-sized object made of wooden slats. It had some complicated machinery, wheels and gears, at one end. Not a rack, surely, thought Celeste, and put it out of her mind. The room was bare otherwise, with a tatty old carpet in the middle of the floor, on which stood a sort of capstan under the dangling ropes. Cockburn was on his knees, throwing open the chests. In one was a jumble of costumes, which he rummaged through, bringing out a jaunty brown hat with a wide, upturned brim and two orange feathers. In another was a heap of implements – whips, flat wooden objects like small spades, and old brass chains and other detritus. He threw an armful of these on to the floor. Then he brought the hat over to Celeste and put it on her head. 'Puss in Boots! You're my Puss in Boots!' he exclaimed. She remembered his fairy-tale obsession, and realised that she must have had the puss-in-boots syndrome in her unconscious when she chose her outfit that morning.

'So – now you are going to tell me about your fantasies,' she said in a firm tone, taking off the hat and putting it on a chest. 'What on earth do you do with all these things?' She had a fairly good idea, in fact, but she held her clipboard busily at the ready, as if to note his reply. Cockburn looked at her appraisingly.

'It is easier to enact my fantasies than to describe them,' he said, 'but I need your help.' Being deliberately obtuse, Celeste asked 'What sort of help?'

'You look like the broad-minded kind of woman. If you were to undress a little, I'd show you. Don't worry, I shan't rape you.'

'I didn't think you would,' she replied with acerbity.

The only way to find out about Cockburn, in the last analysis, was to string him along, and she was intrigued by the whole situation, so she began to undress with a good grace. While she did so, passages from some of his books floated into her memory. He was keen on naked girls being publicly exhibited and humiliated, for one thing. No doubt that was why his poor secretary had to take dictation naked and shivering. He was also extremely enthusiastic about spanking and beating. She slowed down the speed at which she was unbuttoning her jacket and asked Cockburn if he planned to undress too.

'Certainly, that's part of the fantasy.' He was wearing a tweedy sports jacket and flannel trousers with a greenish shirt. He took off the trousers but seemed inclined to keep the shirt and jacket on.

'Fair's fair,' said Celeste. 'Either we both undress, or

neither of us does.' She was not going to have him play the part of the half-dressed French aristocrat. She knew quite well that naked people are powerless people, and she did not intend to be uniquely powerless in this situation. She timed her disrobing to make sure they were both stripped at the same moment. Cockburn was looking at her fine body and a mixture of feelings played across his face. She recognised lust, repugnance and greed, but there were also others. His body was much as she expected – whitish and scrawny, with a small paunch. His genitals were on the small side and almost concealed by his legs, since he stood with them partly crossed. The sight of her generous curving breasts and curled tawny maidenhair had not the effect on Cockburn's penis to which she was accustomed. Instead of embarking on an accolade, he picked up one of the small wooden spades and came over to her. He struck her with it smartly across the rump, and then did it a second time.

Outwardly, Celeste remained unmoved, although her buttocks were stinging; she even managed a wry smile to encourage him to do worse. Inwardly, she was seething. No one spanks Celeste Arden and remains unscathed, she vowed.

'I'm glad you didn't mind that,' he said, though with no obvious sign of delight. 'Now I'll show you something else, if you come over here.' He pointed to the centre of the room where the ropes hung down from the hooks. They went and stood beneath them and he pulled on a rope which ran over a wheel above. A noose descended to within a few inches of Celeste's nose. For the first time, she felt extremely worried and a pulse began to beat in her forehead.

'Sade has influenced me a lot, you see. I find the idea of a young woman strung up naked and helpless, as the plaything for my fancy, most arousing.'

Celeste looked down and saw that he certainly showed signs of arousal. The grey-pink knob of his winkle was peeping out at the top of his legs. He took the noose in his hands and moved towards her. She stepped a pace backwards, quite casually, playing for time.

'You know, I would really like to string you up and play with you,' he said, advancing again.

'Why don't you show me how it's done first? Then I'll know what I'm in for!' She decided to be masterful, otherwise she would very likely let herself in for the sort of degradation which Cockburn liked to lavish on his heroines, and she was not prepared to endure that, even in the cause of Science. She walked up to him again and playfully took the noose from his hands. Curiously, he didn't resist. She pulled it down a little, brought it over his head and looped it round his waist, then pulled it tight. Cockburn's face expressed bafflement and excitement by turns. Celeste moved suddenly away from him and grasped the capstan handle. This operated a gigantic wheel on the end of a drum. She wound it manfully, saying 'So this is how it's done?'

He was a moderately heavy man, but the combination of wheel and gears enabled her to raise his weight with little effort. He was fairly jerked up into the air. She bent and fastened the rope to a ring on the floor, obviously intended for that purpose. Cockburn was now hanging from the waist, his feet and head hanging down towards the floor, and his cock at the level of her chin. He seemed passive as he watched her, but his cock was rising slowly. There were other smaller nooses dangling in the air, and

Celeste guessed their function. She reached two down and put one round each of Cockburn's ankles, and then another which she passed beneath his neck. During this ritual, neither of them spoke, but the tension filled the room like a fog. Each small noose was duly tightened, its rope was hauled on and suddenly Cockburn was hanging in the air as if he were lying in an invisible hammock, but his legs were pulled wide apart, so that all his equipment was visible to Celeste, and prey to her fancy.

Celeste was the first to speak. 'Let me tell you what your fantasies are,' she said with calm ferocity. She was remembering very clearly the various atrocities which he had perpetrated on paper, on victims strung up as he now was.

'First of all, you like to be tweaked – hard.' She reached up between his legs to grip and squeeze his balls, making him flinch and squirm. She ground them in her palms for a time, then reached over the top of his leg and grabbed his swelling prick. By now it was almost erect, but it yielded as she bent it viciously between thumb and fingers. Now he began to moan, but it was not a moan of pleasurable excitement.

Then she retrieved the wooden spade and set about him, thrashing his buttocks noisily and mercilessly from beneath until they were bright red and smarting. He started to whimper: 'No more, please, please stop.'

'But you like the idea of people being beaten till they scream for mercy, don't you?' replied Celeste innocently, still plying the spade. 'So I know that you're just play-acting when you beg me to stop.' She laid into him again with renewed vigour and he shrieked some more. Celeste stopped, not because of his cries, but because there was a danger that she might begin to enjoy the whole charade as an act of revenge, which she did not wish to do. What next? she wondered.

A sort of tube lying on the floor in the heap of artefacts caught her eye. It was bright red plastic, the size and shape of a cock. She remembered a scene from *Cinderella's Betrayal* where Buttons, trussed up like a chicken, had been buggered with just such an instrument. She seized it and went back to Cockburn. Kneeling beneath him, she prodded it upwards into his arsehole.

'STOP! Don't do that!' he screamed, with real fear in his voice.

'But you do like the idea of buggering little boys hung up from hooks on the ceiling, don't you? So why not?'

'No, I hate it, it's a vile idea!' he protested, weakly she thought.

'Then why do you write about it?' asked Celeste. She had given away the secret now.

He didn't reply, so she hardened her heart and shoved the dildo into him. It was quite an easy passage – she imagined it had been up there before. In any event, she only thrust the implement in a short way, not really wishing to harm the man. It was humiliation – his favourite concept – that was uppermost in her thoughts. She jiggled the dildo round and round and from side to side. For a time he jerked and strained against his ropes, but suddenly he went limp and quiet. She stopped and looked at his face. It was flushed scarlet and there were tears on his cheeks. It was not pain, but deep shame that was written there.

She rounded the session off by tickling a few unprotected and highly sensitive portions of him with a feather duster which was among his treasures, and then giving him a short, brisk lashing across the belly with a riding crop. She knew that she had not wielded it hard, for it had left no marks, but he was wailing as piteously as if she had flayed him alive. She noted as a matter of scientific interest that he must have come at some stage. His cock was limp again and there was spunk on his thigh. 'Hours on task: 1, orgasms: 1 (subject)', she noted mentally for her pro forma. She decided now that she had made her point – and she was feeling distinctly sick again.

Her next step was to dress herself quickly. Although she did not think that he had it in him to take a violent revenge and inflict similar woes on her, she thought she would be safer that way – he was less likely to try to string up a fully clothed victim. He twisted his head to watch her and called out, in a grating voice: 'You bitch! You bloody bitch!'

'I've been called worse,' said Celeste cheerfully. 'Now, shall I leave you strung up here for your secretary to find you? I expect she would find it amusing, to say the least. Or shall I let you down if you promise to be a good boy in future?'

'Go to hell,' he growled. Celeste made for the doorway and reached the staircase. 'I'm off down my beanstalk.'

'All right, don't go, I promise . . . Please untie me.' He sounded abject enough at that moment, but she couldn't trust him. Just then, however, she heard a door slam downstairs. So someone else was around, or the servants were back.

'I'll let you down and wait downstairs for you in the hall. As you'll appreciate, the interview isn't quite finished yet. I'd like to know how you feel about your fantasies now. But you may need a few minutes to recover before we go on.'

She lowered the ropes so that he could just about stand on tiptoe on the floor, and left him to free himself. Going down to the study, she collected her briefcase. She paused to place a copy of DFW on his desk. She quickly inscribed it: 'From one pornographer to another. In memory of an afternoon of suspense.' He would be surprised, because he clearly had no notion that she was herself an erotic novelist; none of his rivals' works had found a place on his shelf of paperbacks. She hastened down the staircase to the hall, where she could hear the clattering of plates. The room was brightly lit now, and a very pretty woman, with brown wavy hair and big, liquid brown eyes, was carrying in a tea-tray. She was about thirty, Celeste thought, and remarkably sexy in her way. She was dressed smartly though conventionally, in a flowery summer dress, and she did not have the appearance of being the housekeeper.

'Hello,' said Celeste. 'I'm Celeste Arden. I've just been interviewing Mr Cockburn. He'll be down any minute.'

'I'm really pleased to meet you. I'm Emma – Mr C's secretary,' said the girl, coming over to shake hands. 'I knew you were seeing him this afternoon. He told me to take a couple of hours off, but I decided to come back and make tea for him. He does like tea – tea with crumpets, even in summer.'

'Can I have some too? It's quite a long drive home, and I'm dying of thirst.'

'Of course.' The girl poured out some tea and passed over the plate of crumpets.

They sat companionably together, at one end of the long table. Emma had a bright, frank way of talking. It was hard to imagine her putting up with Cockburn's whimsies and cruelties.

'You're doing a project on sexual fantasies, aren't you? I don't suppose you found Mr C very interesting. I doubt if he ever had one in his life! You'd much better have asked me!' She chuckled.

Celeste realised with a shock that Emma could know nothing of Cockburn's double life. Extraordinary! 'Well, actually, he does have some. If you'll forgive my mentioning it, he said that he dictates his books to you while you sit by the fire stark naked.'

'No, he never did! What a whopper! I didn't realise that he had such imagination.' Emma burst into great peals of laughter.

'And would you believe,' continued Celeste, buttering her next crumpet, 'that he has a torture chamber on the second floor of the turret with all sorts of ropes and pulleys and a rack?'

'Oh, I've been up there often enough. It's the way we get on to the roof when it's sunny. There's nothing up there much except some old chests, where he locks away his manuscripts. The ropes and things are left over from Victorian days when they used it to hang up hams and stuff like that. And the rack was for drying apples and making cider. That's what Mr C told me.'

A very dark horse indeed, this Cockburn, thought Celeste. She tried one more line.

'But what about all those engravings in the room up there?'

'What engravings? There aren't any pictures up there. I think Mr C meant to put some up, because he put up hooks. Maybe he'll get round to hanging up some pictures one day, but he's always so busy writing.'

'How long have you worked for him, Emma?'

'About seven years. Before that, I worked for four years in a City company. I hated that – the men were always making passes at me. Mr C's so different, he's a real gentleman. That's why I stay here – and living in the village is nice too. I've got a cottage there, with a big garden.'

Celeste had finished her tea and had eaten all Cockburn's crumpets. She heard some noises from the tower end of the house and decided to make good her escape.

'I really must dash back to London now – I'm late already. Sorry I can't stay to say goodbye to Mr C, but do tell him that he was a first-rate interview subject. Oh, and please ask him to remember to send me the invoice for his fee. By the way, if you ever want to move back to London, get in touch. I've got just the job for you in my organisation. Here's my card. Thanks so much for the tea. Goodbye!'

As the door closed behind her, Celeste heard footsteps running down the stone staircase. But she was into her car and roaring away down the gloomy drive before Mr Cockburn reached the door. He stood staring after her, red in the face still, looking both angry and wistful. Celeste drove back to London in a superbly cheerful frame of mind, pondering on the astounding Queerness of Folk.

15

Love Knots

When Celeste rang John Smith, or JS as she always called him, to announce his first assignment he was delighted and even agreed readily that the subject for interview should come to his house since her boyfriend might object to his visiting her at home. 'She's a lovely girl, I believe,' said Celeste, gritting her teeth, 'and she has some really original ideas about male and female fantasy which I'd like you to check out.' She then called Lilac to tell her that Mr Smith had agreed to be interviewed at his house near Holland Park in two days' time.

'He's made an extensive study of women's fantasies already, but I think you'll find he has plenty of his own.' Celeste knew this to be true. Her final call was to Véronique, to fix up for her to be present to observe and report on the interaction of JS and Lilac. This task suited Véronique's sense of humour, and anyway she was pleased to be able to start work. She was also delighted to have an excuse to invade John's town-house at last; usually she only saw him at night, in his flat by the canal in Little Venice. She followed Celeste's instructions to the letter and rang John to announce that, on Celeste's say-so, she would be going along to help him with his first interview. She then rang Lilac to tell her that she would try to turn up on the day in case she needed any assistance.

Two days later, Véronique arrived at a smart house in Campden Hill Road, the sort that is described by agents as 'a deceptively spacious artisan's cottage' and costs you half a million. The door was opened by a young man with a smooth, expressionless face and dark hair sleeked back, wearing striped trousers, a tail-coat and a white tie. Being unused to the notion of the English butler, Véronique imagined this to be fancy dress and was not impressed. She was dressed fancily herself, having blown all of her £200 allowance on one garment, a flowing crêpe-de-chine dress with a bold pattern of black and scarlet.

'His Lordship is expecting you, Madam.'

Véronique was startled. *'Mon Dieu! Ce n'est pas un milord?'* she muttered to herself. She was shown into a large garden room where JS sat at his desk, writing out cheques. He rose to give her a perfunctory kiss: she could see he was slightly nervous and not best pleased to have her invade his house. Nevertheless, he was pleased to see Véronique dressed elegantly for once, much as he delighted in her habitual slovenliness. She suggested to him that the best arrangement would be for her to sit out of sight in the sunny garden and to be within earshot of the conversation and on call if help were needed. He installed her there and the butler brought her a long cool drink.

Not long after, the doorbell rang again and Lilac was shown in. She and John shook hands and looked at each other warily.

'It's the prettiest room I've ever seen,' said Lilac, waving her hand round at the conservatory. The sun was flooding in and bringing joy into the lives of the palms and ferns which his interior landscape gardener had insisted on. Lilac too was given a drink to cool her down. She was dressed coolly anyway, wearing a pair of tight silk shorts with sandals, and a matching silk bolero the colour of faded denim. She had somehow gained the impression that JS liked sporty girls. She certainly looked both sporty and sporting, with her cornucopian bosom straining against the fragile satin and her long brown legs stretched out so as to show her finely muscled calves. Soon she was comfortably extended on a canvas *chaise-longue*, with JS in a white wicker chair facing her. She was wondering how to begin the interview when he asked her, 'Are you married?'

'No – not yet, anyway. Are you?'

'No,' he said. 'And, by the way, are you attached to anyone at the moment?'

'Yes. I have a boyfriend – we've known each other for five years or so. Do you have someone too?'

'Not really,' said JS. Véronique, sitting a few feet away but concealed behind a bank of yuccas, sat bolt upright and scowled.

From the perspective of the other two, the interview was going swimmingly, except perhaps for their propensity to throw each question back again at the other. They both admitted to reading pornography – Lilac untruthfully, but she thought this would make for feelings of solidarity and hence a better interview. John was rather surprised when she asked if he went to prostitutes: this girl seemed to have telepathic knowledge of the questions in his mind. Of course, he had planned

207

to omit the question about tarts in Lilac's case. But he in turn answered truthfully that he had extensive experience of prostitutes and had even written about it. Lilac mentally ringed, 'Yes'. She had not brought the questionnaire with her because, with a memory as good as hers, she thought it was unnecessary, and would detract from the spontaneity of the occasion.

'Do you have any special fantasies?' she asked, postponing the question about penises.

'Oh yes, I certainly do. And by the way do *you* ever fantasise?' Lilac nodded.

'Why don't you tell me about them?' they both said in unison. Then they both laughed.

'You first,' said JS, 'after all, I'm asking the questions.' What on earth does he mean? wondered Lilac.

'No, really, I'd love to hear yours,' she said. Her eyes were so big and limpid, so innocent, that JS moved his chair closer and put a hand on her knee, forgetting his duty to obtain information impartially. Her knee was round and dimpled, and warm and silky to the touch.

'My dear young lady, my fantasies would probably sound very boring beside yours. Won't you tell me about them?'

Lilac was adamant. 'Yours first!'

'Oh well, here goes then.' He paused to reflect for a moment.

'One of my fantasies is to take an unknown young lady up to my bedroom during an interview and to make love to her, very gently at first. I would undress her, then stroke her all over, and rub some oil into her skin while she lies, helpless with desire, on my bed and gazes up at me with great, limpid green eyes.'

Véronique was stung by this, because her eyes were muddy brown. She snarled quietly. Lilac looked round to see if there was a cat in the garden, but no cat.

'And what about yours, my dear?' asked JS.

'Oh, mine? Much the same sort of thing,' said Lilac vaguely, hoping to encourage him to go on. JS's hand now rested on her thigh. This was a good sign, and she responded by covering it with hers. He bent forward and kissed her lightly on her cherub's lips, and they seemed to quiver as he did so.

'Do you want to see if real life is as good as fantasy?'

'Oh, yes please,' said Lilac, playing her part for all she was worth.

Taking her hand, JS led her upstairs and into a bedroom which extended right across the house. The whole room was cream-coloured, from the deep furry carpet to the vast king-sized bed. Lamps with fringed lampshades in creamy satin stood on the mantelpiece and dressing-chest, though there was no need of them now, with the sun streaming in. Through an arch in one corner of the room, Lilac could see a round, sunken bath with gold taps. She turned to JS, who put his arms round her and undid the buttons down her back. As her bolero slipped forward, he bent down to press his lips gently to her exposed breasts. He covered them with kisses and she felt her nipples become aware and taut when his mouth brushed against them. His hands sought the fastening of her shorts and soon they too fell to the floor. She stepped out of her sandals, and JS stood back to admire her. His prick was twitching already, but he knew there was ample time to satisfy its ever-ready lust; delay, with the certainty of eventual gratification was a strong part of any fantasy of his. So he took her and laid her on the bed, arranging her like a painter's model for Venus, and went into the bathroom.

When he returned, he was carrying two jars, and wearing only a small, creamy-coloured towel wrapped round his waist. He was tall and shaped like an athlete, and Lilac noticed how fine and sensitive his hands were as he set down the jars on a shelf by the bed.

'You should relax,' he told her, 'that's part of the fantasy, that you are completely disengaged from real life and like putty in my hands. I need an acquiescent subject, you see.'

She shut her eyes and heard him pour some liquid out of a jar – then there was an amazing slithering sensation, as if she were metamorphosing into a fish. The oil which JS smoothed on to her belly and breasts was cool at first in the warm room, but as his hands massaged it into her skin and pores softly but relentlessly, she found she was as hot as if she were wallowing in a bath. JS's questing fingers discovered her secrets one by one – that a circular movement on her nipples made them stand up and swell and blush, and that any touch, however gentle, on the soft, sensitive spot inside her hip-bone made her wince and giggle. After her senses were thoroughly aroused, he moved from her belly to her thighs, deliberately avoiding her pussy. That could come later. When his fingers and palms floated down the muscles inside her legs she began floating, half in a dream: she was a hovering angel fish, and fronds of water-fern were caressing her.

Véronique took her time after the two of them went upstairs, although her inclination had been to follow at once. But she paused to riffle through the papers on JS's desk. There was nothing of note, just some tailor's bills and a bank statement. The size of his credit balance astounded her, and she vowed to make sure that they stopped frequenting wine bars during their evenings together and went somewhere more classy, like Maxim's. There was Celeste's questionnaire with a few annotations such as: 'Follow this one up, might give me some ideas' – beside the power-drill question. She was startled when the young man in the curious clothes came in to clear away the glasses.

'Can I help you, Madam?' he said, staring pointedly at the desk.

'No, I am very well, thank you. I go upstairs to make pi-pi.'

His composure was destroyed for a moment and he almost smiled – then he frowned and went out with the glasses. Véronique went upstairs and soundlessly entered what she guessed was the bathroom via its second door, which led off the landing. She knew she had found the right place, because she heard a soft, sighing noise from the room beyond the arch. Leaving her dress in a heap on top of JS's London suit, she went to the opening and peered out, unseen by the occupants of the room.

JS had turned Lilac on to her front now and was kneeling astride her back, massaging her buttocks with liberal quantities of oil, pulling them apart and letting them flap together again. He squeezed the sumptuous flesh between his fingers with visible relish. His towel had fallen off, and Véronique saw the tool which had so often been her toy standing out between his legs and pointing straight at Lilac's arse. She knew his inclinations too well not to guess what would happen next, especially when she saw him take a large smear of white cream from another jar and smear it into the crease between Lilac's buttocks, then run his fingers lovingly down into the valley beween them. She saw him insert two fingers there with a slow, gentle, prodding movement, and then he bent forward and replaced the fingers with the knob of his bloated cock. Lilac, she guessed, did not sense the difference yet; in any case, she was probably half asleep after her luxurious massage. It had happened to her often enough, Véronique reflected, and she had been duped over and over!

Lilac was still floating in her tranquil aquarium and feeling deliciously sleepy and lazy. There was a funny, tickly, insistent sensation around her buttocks and she felt twinges of a sort she did not recognise somewhere in her loins. She wriggled and twitched a little, before drowsing off again. Suddenly, she felt a sharp intrusion which woke her instantly. Something was inside her, something large and still swelling, and pressed tight against her muscles. But not in her cunt. It moved further inside her and a powerful spasm racked her, and she gave a loud yelp. It ventured further, then withdrew, then went boldly in again, and suddenly she realised what was happening. Lilac had never been assaulted in this way before and the piercing delights of it came as a sweet shock to her. As JS penetrated her with increasing speed and vigour, her control was all gone and she yelped continuously and writhed desperately beneath the delicious onslaught.

JS was on Cloud Nine. He loved a tight, virgin arsehole and his dilating prick was rejoicing in the firm, narrow passage, which he explored now with fierce and erratic thrusts, so as to keep her in suspense and dying and panting for the next sensation – and himself too. The oil he had smeared on his shaft made the incursion easy and Lilac was now totally compliant. After a while, she settled into his rhythm and moaned with joy whenever his prick reached up inside to tweak her tender, untried arse-strings. When these responded with forceful contractions, his organ was gripped and squeezed in a vice-like constriction. Lilac felt the orgasm beginning to well up inside her, spreading out like a web from her anus into her clitoris and ending with great quivering pulses in the wall between arse and cunt, which took her and shook her like a leaf in the wind. She called out again and again and her frenzy spurred JS on to thrust more rapidly until he felt his cock blossoming with delicious slowness and bursting in a shower, in the inmost part of her forbidden passage.

Véronique was shivering with vicarious satisfaction and was hot with desire between her legs and between her buttocks. As JS spent himself and fell forward to lie beside the exhausted, depleted Lilac, she stepped into the bedroom and said, 'Very good, but I too, I want some of that.' Lilac seemed dead to the world and barely stirred, but JS turned his head and grinned a wicked grin and said, 'Don't worry, it's your turn next.' In fact, he could never resist Véronique, with her cheeky rump and brimming tits and her sexy, sluttish ways. He had to limit the time he spent with her in his secret flat, lest he should fall into the final indiscretion and ask her to live with him, so as to have her abundant charms available to him at all times of day. Just now, she was looking especially seductive, her tangled hair tumbling over her shoulders and her tight mango breasts pouting at him and daring him to do the unthinkable. Her legs were glistening smooth, after their first harvesting by her new employer.

213

He slipped off the bed and went to Véronique: taking her by the hand, a finger on his lips, he led her into the bathroom and kissed her passionately, forcing his tongue between her plump lips and licking the top of her mouth. '*Je t'adore*,' he whispered in her ear. '*Sois patiente*.' He washed himself quickly and they made a plan in whispers. Both of them went back to the bed. Lilac had turned towards the middle of the bed. She was sleeping with an angelic smile on her face. JS lay down in the middle facing her, and Véronique lay behind him, her breasts pressing temptingly into his shoulder blades. One of her arms was round him, with a hand languidly palpating the hanging breasts of the sleeping Lilac. JS was titillated by the situation and his prick was hardening and growing.

He insinuated it between Lilac's legs and she stirred and muttered something. When finally she opened her eyes, she felt a stiff rod knocking at the door of her cunt. A hand which was not JS's, for his were round her waist, was teasing her nipples into sharp, tingling prominence. She saw Véronique's hair tumbled across JS's shoulders and realised at last what was happening. Then she opened her legs wide apart and he slipped inside her and began to explore her unfamiliar cunt, hesitantly at first, pausing to let the head of his cock rest against all the unseen fronds and intricacies of her passage, and basking in the damp velvet he found there. Véronique's other hand reached through his legs and fastened itself on his balls. He felt a delicious sense of fullness and ripeness as she cradled them. Lilac was kissing his neck wetly and devotedly and then she wrapped her arms round him and started to fondle Véronique's tits and belly, with soft strokes and tickles. They all moved in unison, like a wave rippling across the bed.

Lilac felt greedy for more pleasure now. She started to exploit JS's strenuous tool by moving herself forcefully against him, driving him further into her than he had intended, and swallowing his prick rhythmically in her deep, voracious cunt. The excitement spread, and he began to move against her strokes rapidly, excavating her deeper than he had thought possible. Meanwhile Véronique took her hand from Lilac's breasts and began to drum on his arsehole entrance with two fingers. He was flooded with sensation in front and behind and was soon panting and laughing as each girl drove him to wilder abandon. The corkscrew motion of his prick had brought Lilac to the plateau of delight and she was flooding his cock with sweet juice. Then he pushed her over the precipice and she was calling out and grasping him tightly round his thighs and pulling him on to her again and again before her cries subsided.

JS would gladly have spent himself there and then – indeed, it was a miracle that he did not, with Véronique's insistent fingers sending his arse wild and with the fierce pumping which his cock received as Lilac's cunt-walls contracted. But he was aware of Véronique's rampaging desire and her hot temper. So when Lilac was quiet and relaxed again, he moved lightly up and over Véronique and pushed her closer to Lilac. Their tits were squashed together, flattened slightly so that they swelled outwards, and Véronique's fingers reached down to bury themselves in Lilac's maidenhair, searching out her hooded shaft of pleasure. JS had hold of Véronique's waist and moving down the bed a little he brought his stiff, over-ripe cock up between her legs and through her pussy-folds which were spread wide apart and voluptuously soft, engorged with blood. He entered her with a fierce rush of desire. As his strokes became more urgent and more lusty, Véronique's magpie fingers pecked at whatever they found between Lilac's legs – the soft tip of her clitoris, the open throbbing mouth of her cunt and her puckered arsehole, still quivering from the delight of violation. Lilac was in overdrive – she was transported by sensual pleasure. With no restraint left, she was on the brink of coming all the time. Within minutes she was jerking her hips and singing out as the new shock-waves spread through her cunt from the other girl's fingers. JS was excited further by his indirect role in Lilac's outpouring and soon felt his own orgasm approaching like a great beast with a cavernous mouth, ready to devour him. But he waited as long as he could, quelling his cock's urgency and haste by retarding and lengthening its strokes, until he was shafting Véronique with the span and vigour of an oarsman. The deliberation with which his swollen, massive organ reached into her soon made Véronique's cunt twitch and burst into song, and she floundered wildly about while he gave a last despairing thrust before his joy overwhelmed him and he shot a cascade into Véronique's palpating, tremulous cunt.

They lay for a while, exhausted, running their hands over each others' sweating, satiated bodies, not knowing which piece of tender flesh or which hand belonged to whom. When finally they unravelled their love-knot and drifted apart, three separate bodies again, JS got up and put on a bath-robe and went down to the kitchen to get some more iced drinks, for the midday sun was making the house hot and their troilistic gymnastics had made them hotter still. He took some time to mix the drinks, and when he padded upstairs with three Tom Collinses on a tray, he looked through the bedroom door before he entered and saw a tantalising sight in the huge mirror opposite the bed. Lilac and Véronique were entwined and caressing each other languidly. Lilac's mouth was moving over Véronique's breasts, sucking and blowing at the soft swelling flesh, and her fingers were twisting delicately at the tip of pink which hid beneath Véronique's fair pussy-fur and which, as JS knew, could become long and stiff when stimulated by his tongue. Véronique had reached through Lilac's legs and was playing with the cheeks of her arse, luring them apart and pushing gently at her arsehole. JS watched for some time, unseen in the doorway, enjoying the entanglement of their elegant limbs and the way that their skins contrasted while their touching breasts seemed to merge into one full, generous curve. They were kissing each other on the lips, too, and sighing occasionally. The scene was more erotic than any performance which could have been choreographed. Eventually, his own rising lust propelled him across to the bed and he lay down, on the outside this time and upside down, so that Véronique could receive his prick into her mouth as she loved to do and he could bite at Lilac's bum and poke a finger into her arse, while Véronique stimulated her cunt by thrusting two fingers into it at the slowest speed possible and withdrawing them a millimetre at a time. Lilac's cunt-lips seemed to restrain her fingers and suck them back inside her.

The tension grew again inside each of them; nerve-ends were stretched taut and raw, begging for relief, and when he could feel the two women about to come through their mutual wanking, JS thrust his prick further into Véronique's mouth, while she sucked and nibbled its tight skin. Then he let himself go once more in a final devastating spasm. The throes of pleasure which consumed Lilac and Véronique lasted longer, and they were still trembling and shivering and crying out when his cock was empty and still. But at last they ceased their tremors and unwound themselves and begged him for a cool drink. Véronique suggested a bath. So it happened that, later on, JS had the sensational experience of being bathed by two very naughty ladies in an experimental frame of mind. He was thoroughly coated with soap in his most private parts, and so he begged them to rinse the foam and slime from his prick: they did it with all four hands, and he disgraced himself by coming so violently and prematurely that it shot all over the wall. They all fell about laughing.

Celeste too had some good laughs when she read the various reports of this occasion. The secret was well-kept, so that both JS and Lilac still thought that the other had been the subject of the interview. Lilac's summary read: 'I am still not sure what Mr Smith's fantasy is, I'm afraid, since he seemed to like giving me a massage, making love to my arse, and also making love with two women at once. I'm sorry I couldn't pin him down more, but it all got very confused.' On the form, under Orgasm Count, she had written: 'Sorry, I've forgotten.'

JS had written, 'Although Lilac claimed to have a lot of ideas about fantasies I was unable to elicit what these were, due to a sudden desire on her part to test some of them out on a practical basis.' Under Orgasm Count he had entered: 'Lost count'. Then he had gone off into those pompous ramblings which Celeste remembered from his diary. 'The act of troilism with two women gives their fascination for orifices free rein, since in such an act there are five major orifices available for manipulation by mouth, hand and penis. This enhances the possibilities of intrusion and extrusion. I would like to write at greater length on this for the Project.' Celeste hoped sincerely that he would not.

Véronique, reporting on the behaviour of the other two, concluded: 'The orgasm rate was elevated. Neither seemed to have inhibitions. The addition of another person (female) to their sexual experiment appeared to increase their enjoyment. Having remarked certain tendencies in JS to voyeurism, I propose that you test him further. For example, one might expose him to pornographic movies, to recalculate his orgasm count while he watches. Both the two researchers are sufficiently enthusiastic about fieldwork, in my opinion, but too lax in going through the questionnaire. I cannot exaggerate too much their need of supplementary training.'

Celeste decided there and then to take on the retraining of JS herself.

16

Fame and Good Fortune

Celeste's bedroom was at the top of the house in the room which had once been the attic. There were sloping walls and secret cupboards under the eaves, and in the morning the sun streamed in through two large windows. The room was painted in several shades of yellow and adorned with shiny things – a panel of foil wallpaper with a swirling pattern here, a rack with a pile of glittering hats there. Much of her vast array of clothes was on display around the room, draped on old curlicued hat-stands and brass wall-hooks. It was a cheerful room to wake up in. On this particular morning, Celeste woke up feeling excited. Today was the day of her television appearance. Doktor Müller had been as good as his word and had proposed her for an open forum discussion on sex, to be chaired by the well-known chat-show host, Mike Morency. She was irritated that Müller had insisted that she should bring along one of her research team, since she was unwilling to share the limelight, but after some heart-searching she had agreed to invite Juliette, since she was the most articulate of the bunch, and quite, though not very, photogenic.

While Celeste was enjoying the early morning sun and

running her hand thoughtfully between her legs, as was her habit, there was a knock on her door. Ivo came in, in black vest and black underpants, with a breakfast tray. He'd cut some of her favourite roses, Buff Beauty, from the garden and had put a vase of them in the centre of the tray, beside the coffee, mango and croissants. There was also a folded piece of paper on the tray. Ivo gave her a warm kiss on her forehead and put the tray on one side of the wide bed. Then he sat down on the other to watch her eat, as he loved to do. He was looking stunningly handsome this morning, and Celeste's heart warmed to him again. She unfolded the paper and read:

> There was a young girl called Celeste,
> Who conducted her sex life with zest,
> She liked men to swive her
> While clad like Godiva
> Since her chest impressed best when undressed.

She started heaving with laughter, then Ivo joined in and they were both rolling round the bed together, hugging each other and almost upsetting the coffee jug.

So the day had started well. The morning was spent on doing the year's income tax returns for the accountant to scrutinise, which also occasioned Celeste and Ivo a good deal of innocent merriment as they itemised the various expenses and equipment to be set against tax. Celeste wondered whether the Grackle dildo-seat could be written down as a capital asset. Ivo suggested that it ought to be regarded as base stock. Then it was time to dress for the studio, and she took some time choosing her gear. Juliette was bound to turn up looking tarty, so she eventually decided to look as prim as was possible. She chose a severe long jacket without revers in black satin and tight black silk pants. Under the jacket she wore a deep yellow blouse, and she put a piece of black velvet round the neck, in the semblance of a tie. Short black boots, of course, completed the ensemble. When Ivo had admired her sufficiently – and genuinely – she sent him to get a taxi. The show was being filmed in the afternoon for transmission early that evening, but there was to be a buffet lunch for the participants first.

The lunch was held in a room with huge glass windows on one side, which overlooked the studio. At lunch there were the six panellists, Mike Morency, the producer and various researchers and acolytes; the invited studio audience was not getting the chance of freeloading. Juliette was there, dressed in a glittering sheath of a dress and draped with strings of flashing gemstones. Doktor Müller had dressed for the occasion in a woollen suit with a Hound-of-the-Baskerville's-tooth pattern, to which he had whimsically added a pink shirt and bright orange tie. He greeted Celeste warmly, but with a hint of trepidation, and was anxious to find out which fantasies she planned to talk about. Whose fantasies, more like, she thought, and replied that she would play it by ear. The other panellists consisted of a criminologist called Jules, a sex therapist called Heidrun and an elderly woman, Miss Jameson, who was widely known as the Guardian of Public Morals. Morency bustled around ingratiating himself with his guests and putting them at their ease, Celeste chatted to Juliette and Müller, and after half an hour it was time to get made up. She always enjoyed sitting back in a chair while a girl's soft hands spread cream and powder all over her face, but on this occasion the cosmetics assistant was a young man, Leo. He shaded her eyes with great skill and tenderness and seemed to enjoy the process of gilding the lily. She found the scenario exciting, but there was no time to exploit it.

When the panellists took their seats in the luridly decorated studio, the audience of some twenty respectable-looking men and women, mainly middle-aged, were already seated. Morency explained to everyone the format of the programme and stated the order in which he would call on the panellists for their spontaneous discussion. 'Please don't speak out of turn, or interrupt each other,' he warned. The theme was to be 'Sexual fantasy – do we need it?' Then floodlights were switched on, cameras rolled, microphones descended and there was a call for silence. Morency, a large flabby man with unctuous manners, leered into Camera Number One and said 'This evening's open forum discussion is one on which everyone has something to say – the subject of sexual fantasies. Are they essential to a healthy sex life? Do they lead to or aggravate sexual crimes? Do they corrupt the young people of today? And perhaps the most fascinating question of all – what sorts of fantasies do people have? We have a wide range of experts here who will try to answer these questions, and other questions put by the audience here.'

Introductions were made and the sex therapist was asked first about the role of fantasy. Heidrun appeared to Celeste as if she might be into stern Swedish discipline, but she came across as a wishy-washy individual whose views could be summarised as 'if it turns you on, it's okay'. But she did say that the development and sharing of fantasies between couples could revive a flagging sexual relationship. The criminologist was then adamant that sex crimes were rarely linked specifically with fantasy although, of course, many rapists had fantasies, like everyone else. His view was that a vivid fantasy life would deter, rather than cause, crime. Miss Jameson was invited to pontificate on whether fantasy was a social evil.

'Yes,' she replied without hesitation. 'Fantasies distract us from real life and prevent the fantasy-ridden individual from concentrating on the true purpose of sex, a meaningful and procreative marital relationship.'

'I don't agree,' interrupted Celeste, receiving a warning look from Morency. 'Couple relationships would collapse even faster if the people involved didn't have fantasy as an outlet when things go wrong between them. Have you noticed the divorce rate, by the way?'

Heidrun chimed in too, in her support. Miss Jameson cunningly and imperceptibly changed tack. It became evident that what she meant by fantasy was perversion or fetishism which must, by her definition, be a social and moral evil.

Juliette interjected: 'Surely not. If I have a beautiful dream about fucking my boyfriend on a desert island with blue sea and sun all around us, it makes me feel good and it makes me fuck him better. Is that perverse?'

Morency was frowning and a red light was flashing in the corner of the studio. An assistant appeared, out of the range of the cameras but within sight of the panellists, and held up a hastily written notice, 'PLEASE DO NOT USE FOUR-LETTER WORDS. "MAKE LOVE" IS PREFERRED.'

Morency let the skirmish with Miss Jameson go on for a time because she was a well-loved figure in many drawing-rooms, although well-mocked in many more. Then he interrupted crisply and said, 'Well, now we've looked at the pros and cons of fantasies and there is, I might risk saying, a measure of agreement that fantasies are not entirely a bad thing.' As he paused for breath,

Doktor Müller interjected: 'No, if you please, I think we all agreed they were a thoroughly *good* thing, except Miss Jameson.' Morency looked fed up; he tried again. 'Anyway, let's turn now to look at the content of fantasy. We are fortunate to have with us Celeste Arden, director of the Arden Foundation for Sexual Research, who is currently conducting a massive study of men's sexual fantasies. Also, Juliette, one of her research team. Now, Celeste, what sort of things are fantasies about?'

'They can be about anything really. I could fantasise about Doktor Müller's tie if I wanted to. But if that was all I thought about you might well call it a fetish. I can answer the question best by telling you a few typical male fantasies. There is for example the 'zipless asterisk', meaning sex with a stranger with no strings attached on a one-off basis. There are various kinds of voyeurism: you might dream of levitating while you are asterisking, and looking down on yourself. Or some men prefer to watch other people at it while remaining hidden themselves. Then, nearly all men imagine how it might be to 'f'-word two women at the same time; most of them are especially turned on by the idea of the women having it off together too. Then again, some men are more interested in one particular part of the body than another, and have fantasies about that. I can't really say more about that on the air, but I'll give you a hint – it has something to do with bottoms.' There were giggles from the audience, the red light was flashing urgently and the camera cut to Morency, who passed the question to Juliette, unwisely.

'As a member of the Arden research team, have you found out about any interesting fantasies?'

'Yes, lots. One of them is the gang-bang. Three young men wanted to have it off with me in turn. And then there's the sort of man who can only get it up by telling you dirty stories. And I once fucked a Catholic priest who insisted on doing it in the confessional. And then, there's politicians: let me tell you about –' There was a disturbance at the back of the studio – the producer was standing up and waving his arms and apparently shouting behind the soundproof glass wall. Morency cut Juliette off brutally in mid-flow and smoothly turned the questioning on to Müller.

'Dr Müller, you are a psycho-sexologist. Can you tell us what makes us fantasise, in the final analysis?'

Müller removed his spectacles and leaned forward, the very epitome of earnestness and Teutonic wisdom.

'*Ja*. Take for example my case. I have always wanted to lie on my analyst's couch and masturbate myself while she watches. What is my motivation? Gratification and release. I need not do this with a real person because I can get great satisfaction from wanking while I think about this scene. To take another example, some men have fantasies about bondage and flagellation, and they have orgasms when they think about this. Their aggression – or submission, if we talk about the masochistic side of the activity – is sublimated through these fantasies, and thus not manifested in any more socially dangerous form. Many pornographic authors trade on this fact. What I would say is that the sexual drive is there in all of us, but in some people it gets fused with some other part of the personality, or associated with a past experience, like breast feeding or toilet-training. After this fusion, it comes out as a particular kind of fantasy. Take for example the judge who wants to fuck wearing his robes: each person's particular fantasy also provides an outlet for some other side of the personality as well as for his or her sexuality. For these reasons fantasies are as varied as people.'

Celeste had been listening intently – Müller was making sense at last. Morency now threw the subject open to the audience, but there were only a few minutes left. One questioner had to be restrained because, when the camera was on him, he seemed to want to get out his fantasy and show it to the viewers at home. A man asked Miss Jameson whether she had any proposals for criminalising fantasy, and raised a laugh. Then a studious-looking woman asked Celeste: 'In your research, how do you know that men are giving you truthful answers? I certainly wouldn't tell anyone what my fantasies are.'

Celeste had prepared a euphemistic answer for just such an emergency. 'My researchers are fully trained in ways of eliciting the truth. They cross-check one answer against another and follow up any discrepancies. There is an element of empirical research to ascertain whether there has been prevarication and to verify the truth of some of the responses.'

'In other words,' added Juliette, 'we fuck them to make sure they're not lying – or bugger them, or whatever turns them on.'

The programme ended in some confusion. Half the audience was laughing audibly and drowning Morency's platitudinous closing words. Miss Jameson was seen to wag her finger threateningly at Juliette and the camera caught Juliette's response, which was to stick out her tongue and put her finger up her nose. The microphone also overheard Doktor Müller asking Celeste, 'could you really fetishise my orange tie? *Sehr interessant!*' After they had escaped from the studio – and no one seemed inclined to detain them to sign contracts for future appearances – Celeste and Juliette and Doktor Müller went off to console themselves with a bottle of wine in a drinking club in Mayfair. Müller turned out to be a talented mimic: he took off all the panellists in turn, including Celeste with her mixture of assertiveness and nervousness, and he was especially good at being Morency exuding banalities. Celeste could see that Juliette was becoming increasingly fascinated by him, and so, generously deciding to leave them to research each other, she made an excuse and left.

Back home, Ivo had been spending the afternoon in the kitchen, cooking a special celebration supper for Celeste. He made several different sorts of Malaysian curry, grinding all the spices by hand, and a Queen of Puddings. Then he set the table in the dining-room, with candles ready to light. When Celeste arrived, he welcomed her in the hall with a glass of champagne. She was exuberant and told him all about the fiasco at the studio. Then it was time to watch the programme, and they cuddled on the couch while watching and giggling.

Celeste and Ivo were not the only viewers with a personal interest in it. Mr Justice Grackle sat in his sombre drawing room on the edge of his chair, while his wife bustled about tidying the spotless room and tut-tutting whenever a bad word was used. He was racked with a sudden fit of coughing when Dr Müller mentioned judges' robes. 'Excuse me, my dear,' he spluttered, 'I think I'll have to go upstairs for a moment.' Cockburn was watching the programme too, and started to bite his nails when bondage was mentioned, then fell back in his chair with relief as the conversation moved on. He punched a cushion violently whenever Celeste appeared on the screen. Mr Mortimer, slumped deep in an armchair and half-asleep, woke up and listened and nodded sagely, muttering 'Same when I was young. Nothing new under the sun.' And Luciano, in his flat in Bloomsbury, had his eyes riveted to the screen as he saw the girl from the Pleasuredrome appear like a vision, so stunning, so magnificent. He was very disappointed that something seemed to have gone wrong with his television set. Whenever she spoke the sound became inaudible, drowned in a mysterious whistling and crackling of the air waves.

After supper, which Celeste enjoyed heartily and praised lavishly, she invited Ivo up to her bedroom. He was wearing a black boiler suit by way of evening dress, and when she had turned down the lights to a mere glimmer in the corners, she stood in front of him and slowly pulled down the front opening zip. He was kissing her neck and had cupped her satiny buttocks in his hands.

'I love you,' he whispered again and again.

'So, you're not gay after all?' she asked sardonically, as her hands slid through the opening and caressed his smooth flat belly.

'No, I'm sure I'm not.'

Irritation fought with affection in Celeste's emotions and won, as usual. 'Admit it – you are a silly bastard aren't you? It was all self-indulgent trash.' She could not see Ivo's face, since it was still at her neck. But she went on with her caresses, and peeled down his garment. As always, the beauty of his slim young body touched her, and she found she was pressing herself against him like a child against its mother's legs. Ivo sighed, and then began to undress Celeste with tenderness, stopping to examine and plant kisses on each newly exposed part of her. He spent a long time over her succulent breasts, licking the nipples the way she liked, and biting gently at the full curve of their overhang. When he had undressed her completely and they stood together, framed in the great gilded mirror on the wall opposite, he paused to admire her – and himself. Then, holding hands, they went to bed.

Celeste felt quite randy, what with success and champagne and hot curry all coursing through her. She rolled on top of Ivo, upside down, and teased his cock, which was rather subdued for some reason, into a thick towering spire which she kissed and sucked. Her tongue ran round his delicate foreskin and forced it back and she licked and chewed at the darkening knob, and sucked out a drop of his moisture. His hands were holding her breasts, trying to contain and support their weighty fullness, and squeezing them as she moved gently on top of him. He raised his head slightly and put out a long tongue and tantalised her pussy into a state of openness and desire, by drawing his tongue from the tip of her clitoris down across her cunt-lips to where her enigmatic arsehole trembled slightly at the touch.

As they pleasured each other in a leisurely fashion, confident of fulfilment, Celeste's cunt was racked with a fierce appetite for Ivo's cock, and she turned round and spread her legs wide, offering him her moist, welcoming cavern. It devoured his thick long prick with ease and gluttony and soon she felt it work its magic on the walls of her cunt. Her clitoris was roused and went crazy each time Ivo's organ travelled the length of it en route for its dark interior destination. Ivo could feel the strength of her muscles as she clenched her cunt-mouth to delight his cock, and he suddenly wanted to take Celeste finally and totally.

He rolled them both over and lay on top of his mistress and began a bout of wild thrusting which sent messengers running through her whole nervous system. A warm flush spread over her skin and her limbs felt weak as water. She could not resist the impending joy. For Ivo, his delight was all centred in his leaping, plunging cock and so fast did he wield it that he was breathless and gasping, unable to come because of his overwhelming excitement and tension. At the peak of his desperate thrusting, Celeste felt her crisis coming and gave herself up to the turmoil, shouting and hugging Ivo passionately while his magic wand conjured great gusts of pleasure in her loins. Ivo slowed down and almost stopped fucking her for a few minutes, but left his cock lying inside her to fill out her exploded cunt. He kissed her eyelids and cheeks and whispered sweet things while nibbling her ears.

As sensation returned to the swooning nerves of her pussy, she felt Ivo's wand inside her, dilating her passage and pressing against the walls at the sealed gate at its end. She gripped his waist tightly and he came down into her again with measured strokes, lingering inside, pausing outside the mouth of her cunt to frustrate her for a second or two each time. Soon she was begging him to fuck her faster, but he refused and continued his languid incursions until he felt she was ready to be exploded again. Her cunt-juice was bathing his prick and trickling down his balls and he knew she could not last. So he speeded up his strokes and twisted his cock each time he entered, to excite the sensitive muscles around the soft entrance of her cunt. His cock made heavy lunges which soon drove both of them to a fierce frenzy and Celeste was shouting as she came and Ivo was crying as his spunk flooded out of him and his balls contracted to shoot another burst of it into her delectable, convulsing cunt.

After many kisses and sweet words, they fell asleep with their legs entwined. Towards the morning, Celeste dreamed that she was in a room full of mirrors, alone but with a hundred naked images of herself. She did not know which one was her and she felt wretched and tried to avoid seeing herself – or to escape her own scrutiny, perhaps. She found a tiny door between two mirrors and squeezed herself through it and found she was in a beautiful garden, with a stream running through it and a fountain sparkling in the distance. As she walked through the garden, the warm grass pressed up between her bare toes. Then she saw the toad, a giant brown toad crouched on a large rock by the stream and basking in the sun under a lilac tree. On an impulse, she went over and kissed it between the eyes. Its eyes opened wide – they were Ivo's dark eyes. It turned into a man – no, not a man but a playing card, the Jack of Spades, and the Jack walked out of the card towards her holding up his carved and painted wand. He waved it at her – she was frightened, and took a step backwards, and felt herself slipping . . .

When she woke, Ivo was not there. Come to think of it, he had said something about going out early. He seemed to do that a lot these days. Celeste lay and thought about Ivo while the sun climbed steadily up the sky until it lit up her bed. Fucking last night had been wonderful, but underneath it all something was not right. Maybe he was in love with Lilac, preposterous as it might seem. Well, Lilac was more his own age anyway. Yes, he was devoted to Celeste in some way, and she to him, but something in her made her unable to be the uncritical, adoring lover he needed – and, if she were honest, deserved. Before she got up, Celeste had decided that Ivo had better go. She would tell him as soon as he returned.

She breakfasted in a glum mood after this decision, and went to her office with a sense of profound weariness. She began to rummage through the reports, wondering if she would or could ever analyse them into some sort of concluding report, and whether it would be any good anyway. Then the downstairs doorbell rang and she went to answer it. On the step stood a dark, handsome stranger, very dishevelled and panting. He was dressed in black.

'I am looking for Juliette,' he said. His accent was foreign – Italian she thought. 'I see her again on television last night, and find out where she works. I must see her.'

Celeste stalled: Juliette might not wish to see this young man again, whoever he was, and besides he was easy on the eye and she felt like some company. She asked him in, and pretended to have lost Juliette's number. Then she offered him a coffee. He was looking around in wonderment at the strange room, and admiring the masks and asking what the instruments were. He was obviously clever and lively, and had all the charm of his race.

'You know,' he said, 'when I see you last night on TV, I think, here is a really beautiful and astonishing woman – a woman I would love to meet. So I'm glad I am here now.'

Celeste decided that she had really lost Juliette's number. She invited him to stay for lunch.

Some weeks later, Samantha received the following letter:

Dear Samantha,

I can't get back from Italy just yet – indeed, I may be some time. So I wonder if you would care to take on the task of co-ordinating Project Fantasy Uncover? It pays thirty thousand a year! You know the ropes, after all, and can fix up the training too. I hope you'll say yes. If you do agree, remember that Juliette cheats on expenses, and Justine will send in reams of novelistic garbage unless you're very strict with her. You'll find the accounts in good order, thanks to my special arrangement with the accountant. I'll be continuing my part of the project over here, with Luciano's help. I think we missed out on a whole dimension in our earlier research on fantasies – romance! But there's still time for all that – the final Report isn't due for a year. Don't know when I'll be back. Love to you and all the girls, and Ivo if he's around,

Celeste

ADULT READS

ANONYMOUS AUTHORS

0352314850	The Adventures of a Schoolboy	£2.50
0352313269	Beatrice	£2.99*
0352314915	The Boudoir	£2.99*
0352317884	Confessions of an English Maid	£2.75*
0352322152	The Devils Advocate	£2.99
0352317221	Eroticon	£2.99
0352318627	Eroticon II	£2.99
0352321660	Eroticon III	£2.99
0352313374	Eveline	£2.99*

These books are obtainable from many booksellers and newsagents. If you have any difficulty tick the titles you want and fill in the form below.

Name _____

Address _____

_____

Send to: Nexus Cash Sales, P.O. Box 11, Falmouth, Cornwall, TR10 9EN.

Please send a cheque or postal order to the value of the cover price plus:
UK: 55p for the first book, 22p for the second book and 14p for each additional book ordered to the maximum charge of £1.75.

BFPO and EIRE: 55p for the first book, 22p for the second book, 14p per copy for the next 7 books, thereafter 8p per book.

OVERSEAS: £1.00 for the first book and 25p per copy for each additional book.

While every effort is made to keep prices low, it is sometimes necessary to increase prices at short notice. Nexus reserve the right to show new retail prices on covers which may differ from those advertised in the text or elsewhere.

**NOT FOR SALE IN CANADA*

ADULT READS

0352322454	**Forbidden Frolics**	**£2.99**
0352322004	**The French Collection**	**£2.95**
0352317817	**Exploits of a Young Don Juan**	**£2.50**
0352318554	**Flossie**	**£2.99** *
0352313390	**'Frank' and I**	**£2.99** *
0352316667	**Lascivious Scenes**	**£2.99** *
035231530X	**Laura Middleton**	**£2.99**
0352315830	**The Lustful Turk**	**£2.99** *
0352310170	**A Man With A Maid**	**£2.99** *
0352310928	**A Man With A Maid Vol II**	**£2.99** *

These books are obtainable from many booksellers and newsagents. If you have any difficulty tick the titles you want and fill in the form below.

Name _____

Address _____

_____

Send to: Nexus Cash Sales, P.O. Box 11, Falmouth, Cornwall, TR10 9EN.

Please send a cheque or postal order to the value of the cover price plus:
UK: 55p for the first book, 22p for the second book and 14p for each additional book ordered to the maximum charge of £1.75.

BFPO and EIRE: 55p for the first book, 22p for the second book, 14p per copy for the next 7 books, thereafter 8p per book.

OVERSEAS: £1.00 for the first book and 25p per copy for each additional book.

While every effort is made to keep prices low, it is sometimes necessary to increase prices at short notice. Nexus reserve the right to show new retail prices on covers which may differ from those advertised in the text or elsewhere.

*NOT FOR SALE IN CANADA

ADULT READS

0352313781	**A Man With a Maid Vol III**	£2.99*
0352316209	**Maudie**	£2.25
0352314826	**The Memoirs of Dolly Morton**	£2.25
0352313692	**More Eveline**	£2.99*
0352318457	**A Night in a Moorish Harem**	£2.50*
0352311355	**Oh Wicked Country!**	£2.25
0352316756	**Parisian Frolics**	£2.25*
0352320494	**Pleasure Bound**	£2.95
0352315687	**Randiana**	£2.99*

These books are obtainable from many booksellers and newsagents. If you have any difficulty tick the titles you want and fill in the form below.

Name _____

Address _____

_____

Send to: Nexus Cash Sales, P.O. Box 11, Falmouth, Cornwall, TR10 9EN.

Please send a cheque or postal order to the value of the cover price plus:
UK: 55p for the first book, 22p for the second book and 14p for each additional book ordered to the maximum charge of £1.75.

BFPO and EIRE: 55p for the first book, 22p for the second book, 14p per copy for the next 7 books, thereafter 8p per book.

OVERSEAS: £1.00 for the first book and 25p per copy for each additional book.

While every effort is made to keep prices low, it is sometimes necessary to increase prices at short notice. Nexus reserve the right to show new retail prices on covers which may differ from those advertised in the text or elsewhere.

*NOT FOR SALE IN CANADA